ELVIS

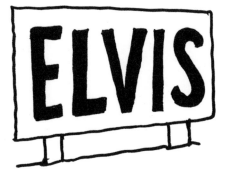

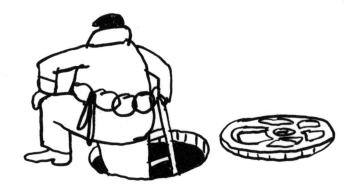

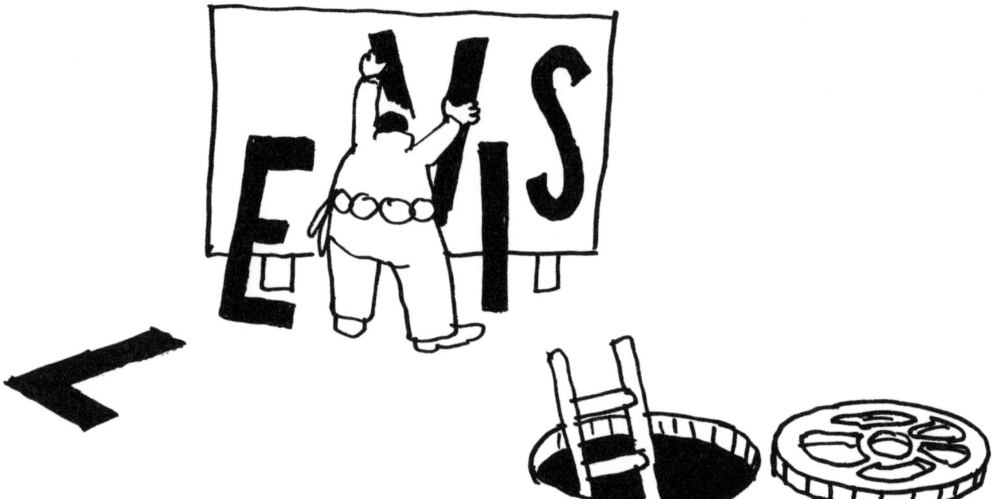
EMIS
L

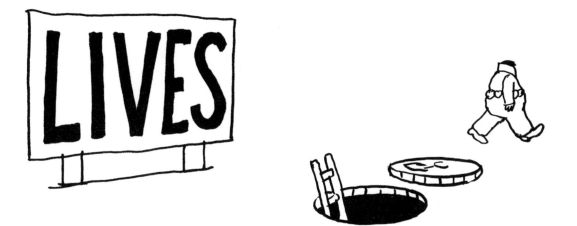

LIVES

and Other Anagrams

Collected and Illustrated
by Jon Agee

Farrar Straus Giroux • New York

To Winced Poet and Tepid Debt*

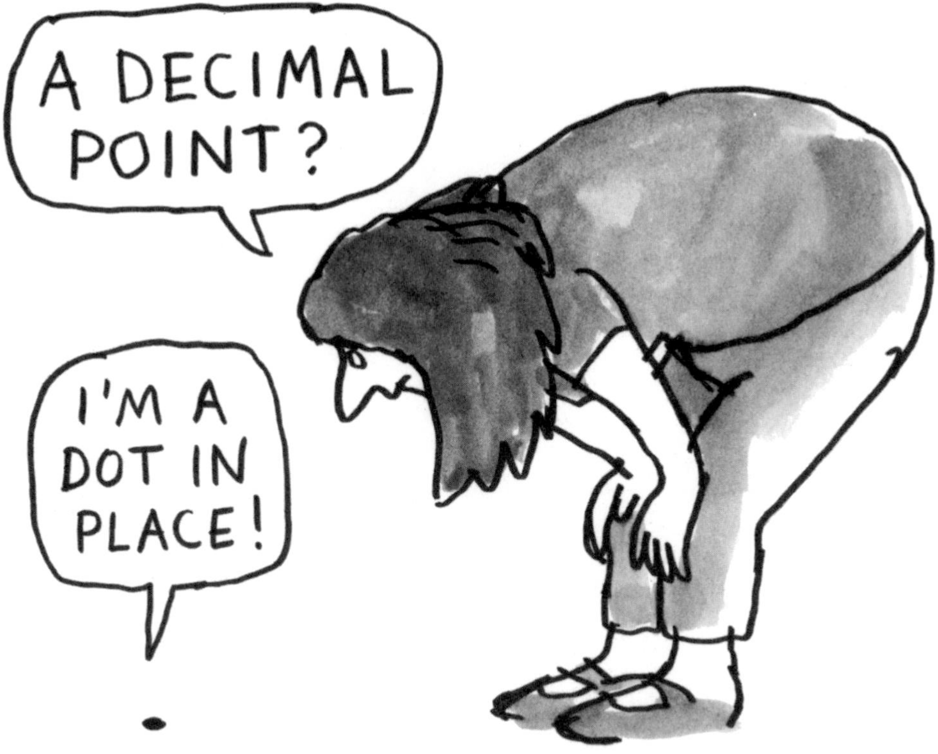
A DECIMAL POINT?
I'M A DOT IN PLACE!

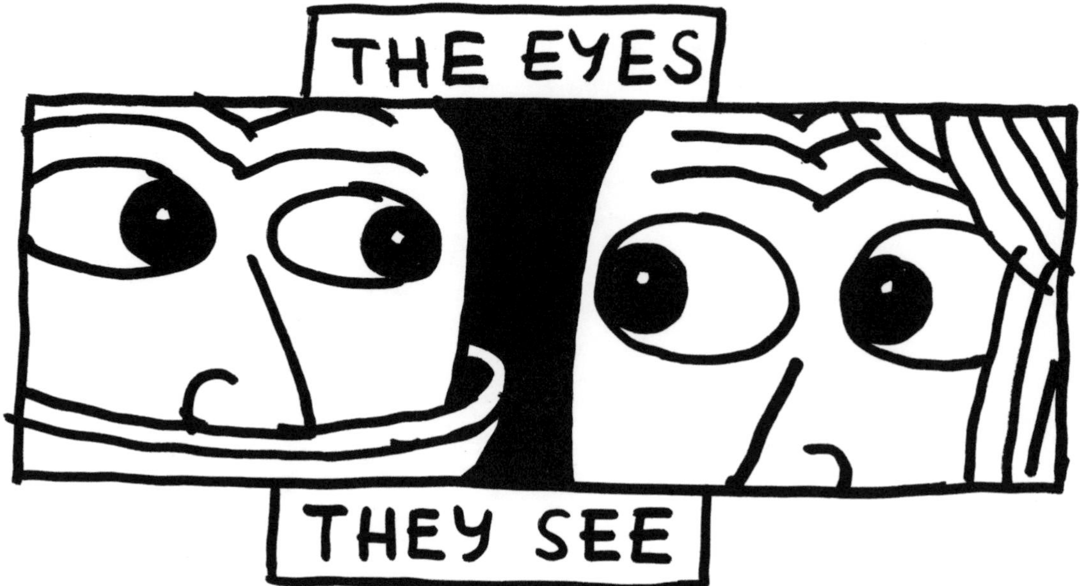
THE EYES
THEY SEE

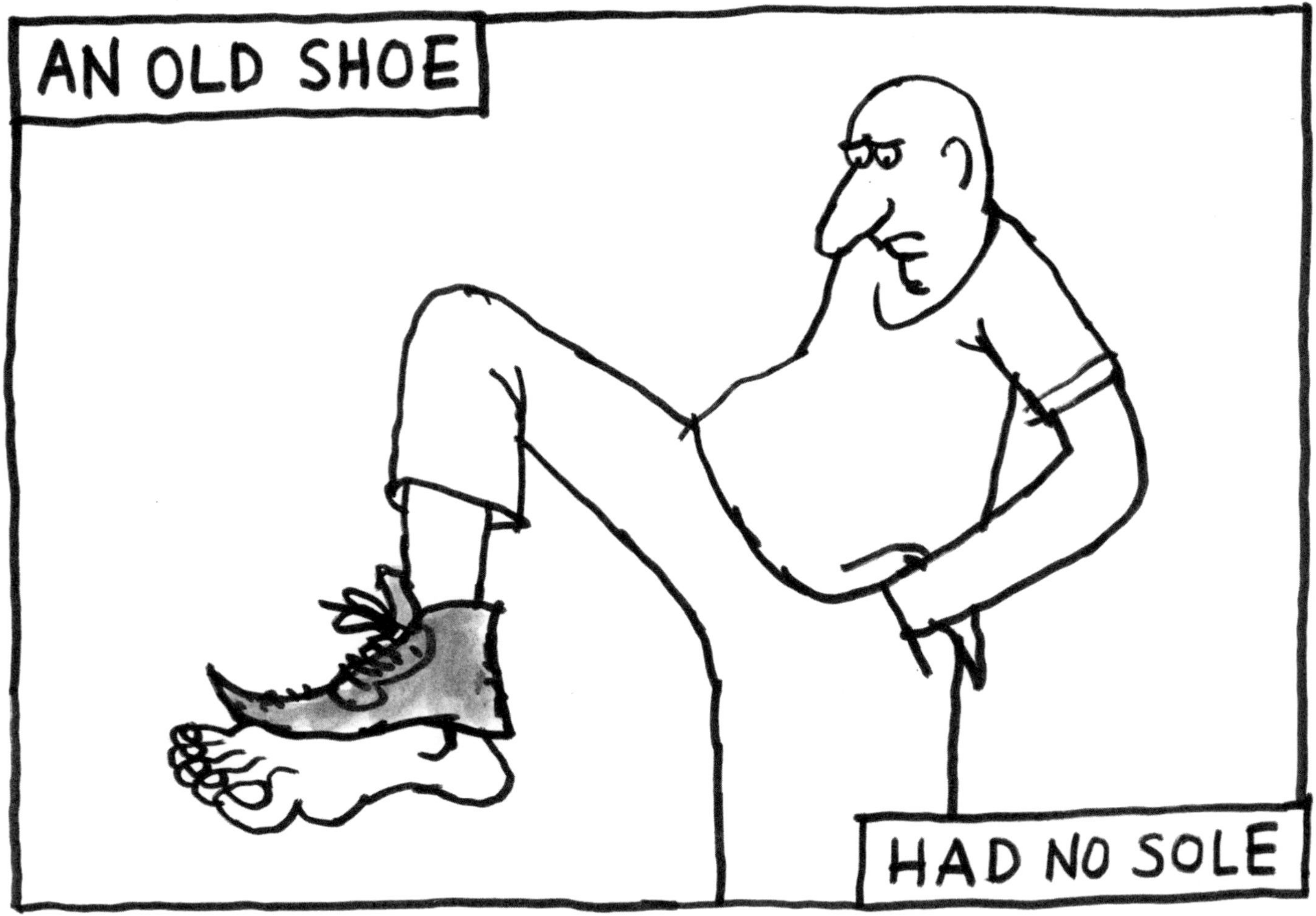
AN OLD SHOE
HAD NO SOLE

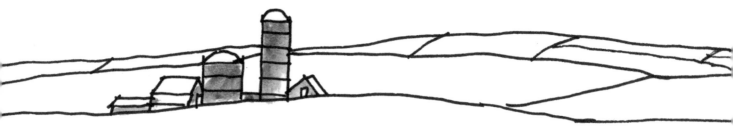

THE COUNTRYSIDE

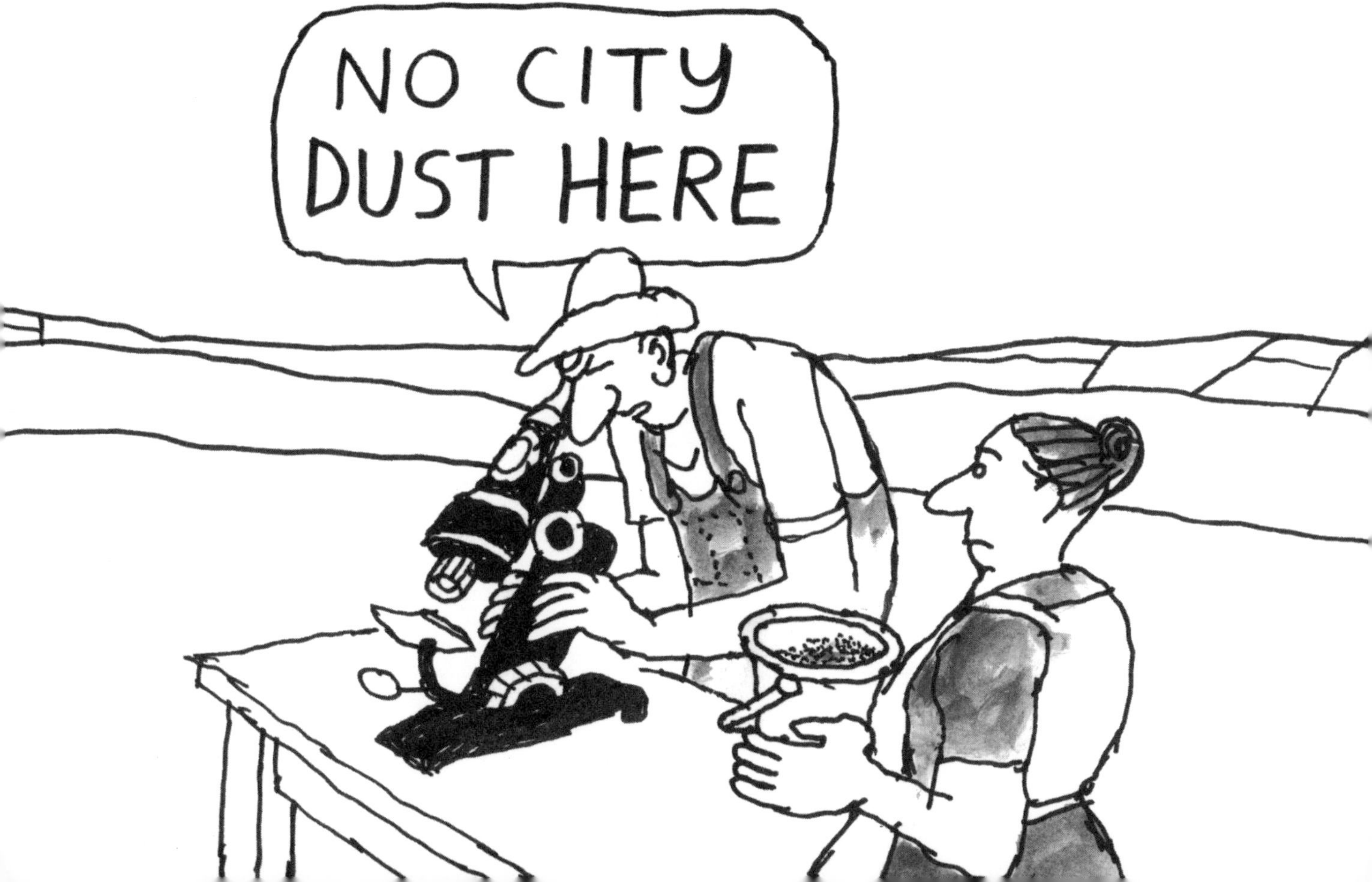
NO CITY DUST HERE

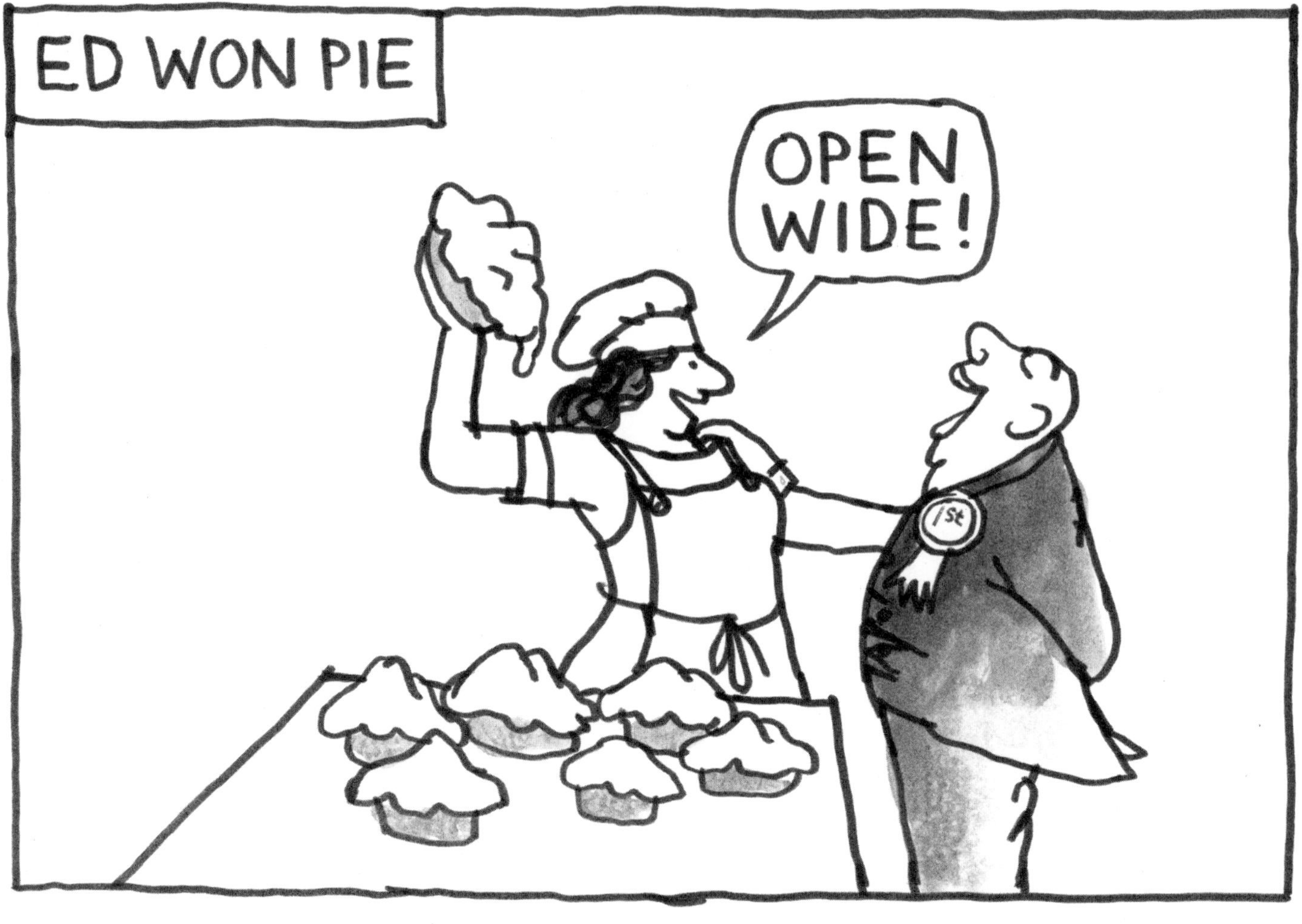
ED WON PIE
OPEN WIDE!
1st

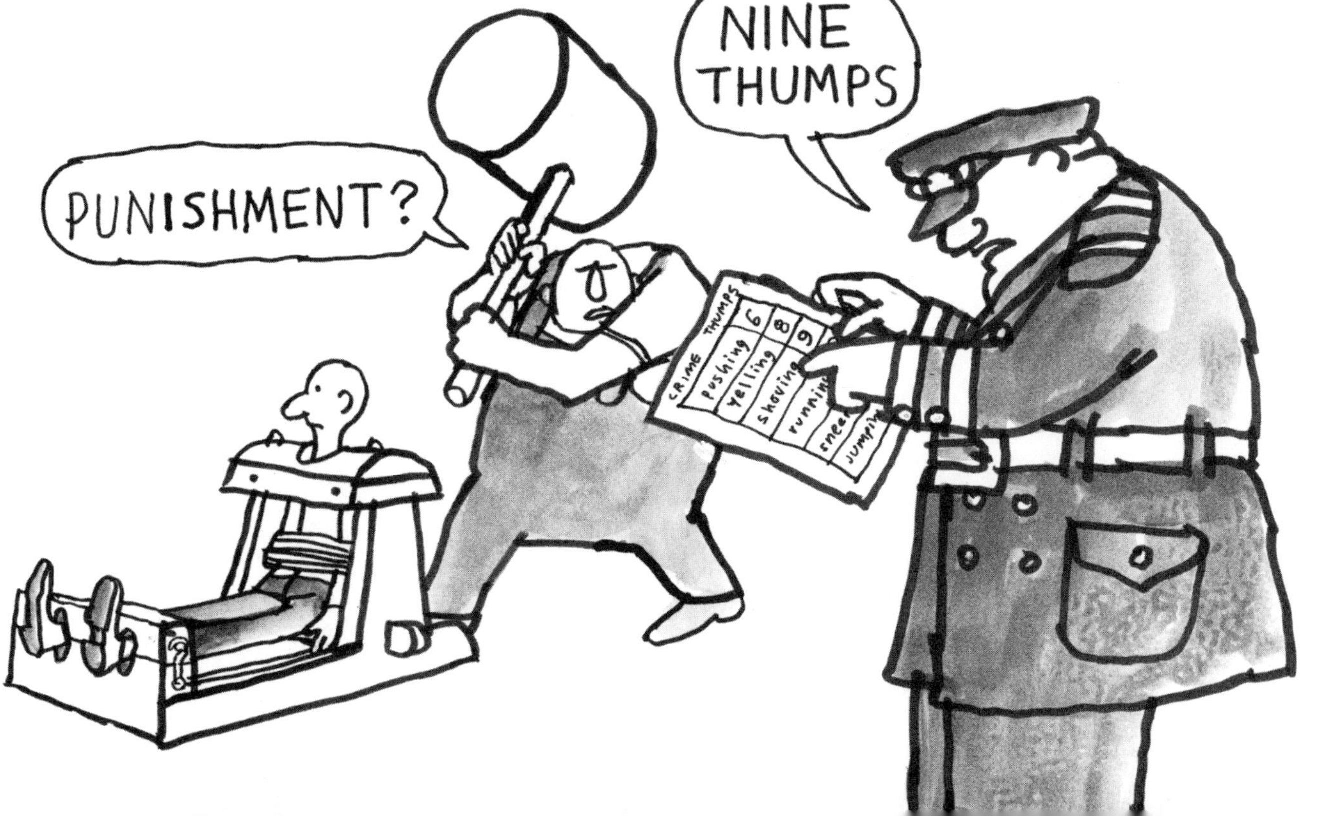
PUNISHMENT?
NINE THUMPS
CRIME
THUMPS
pushing
6
yelling
8
shoving
9

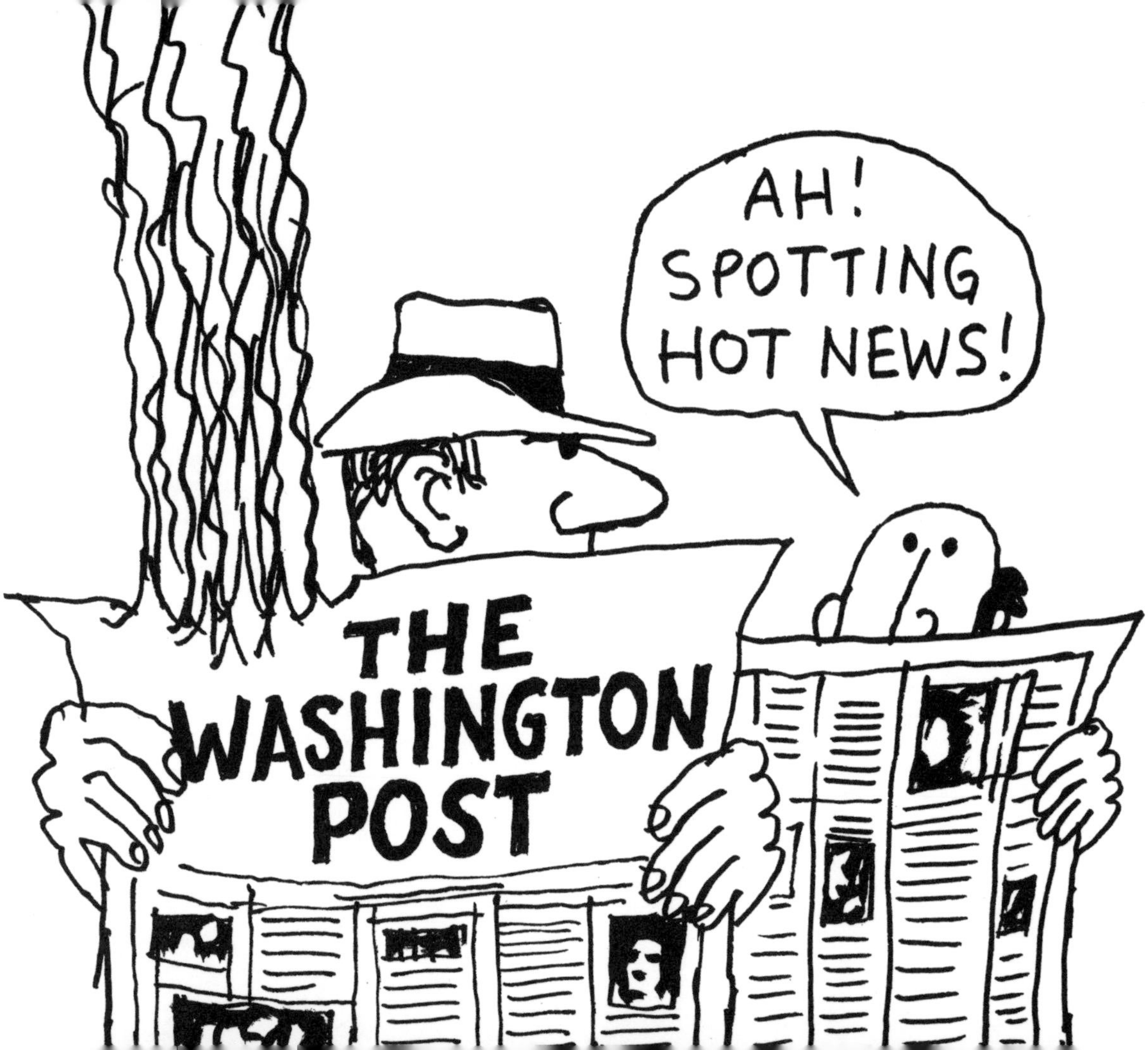
AH! SPOTTING HOT NEWS!
THE WASHINGTON POST

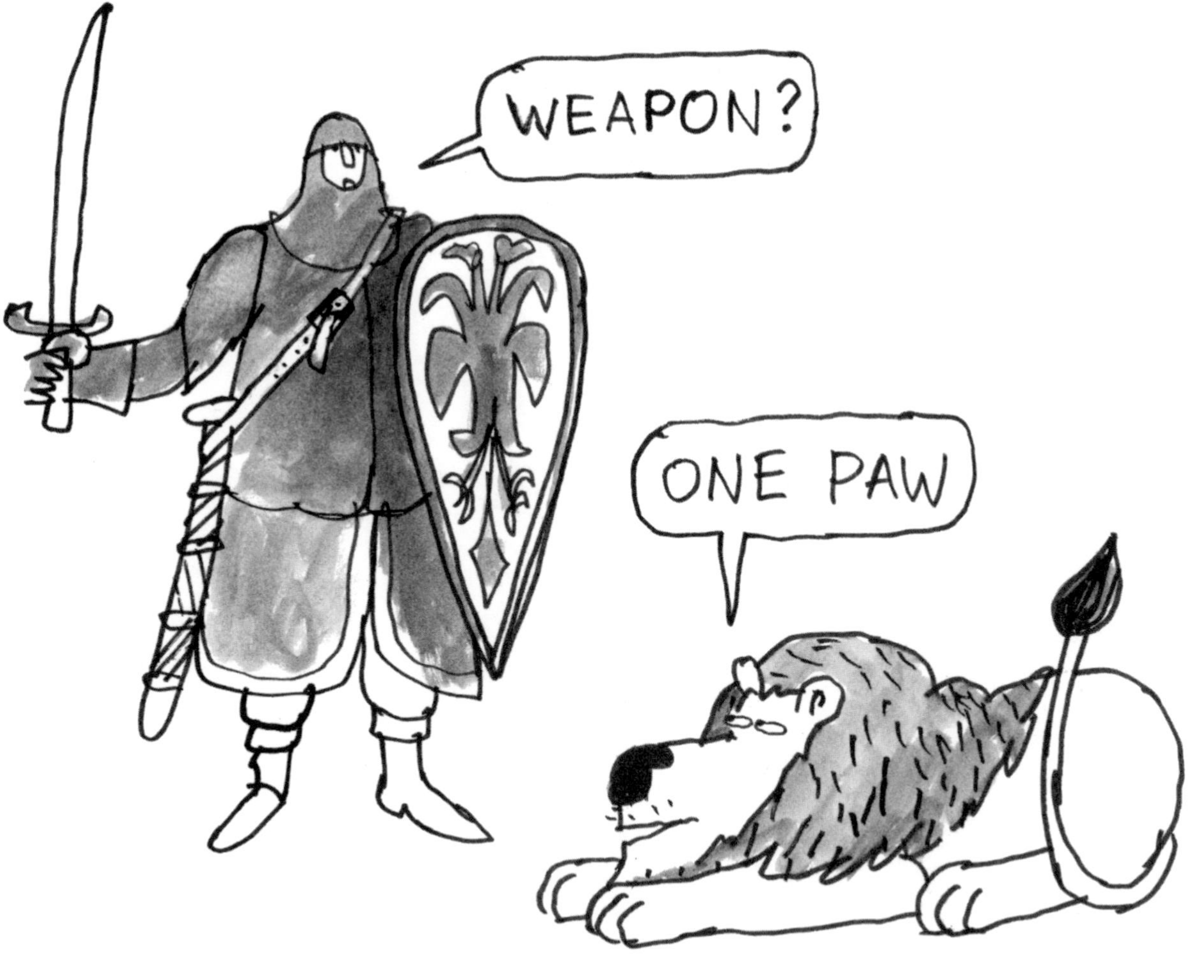
WEAPON?
ONE PAW

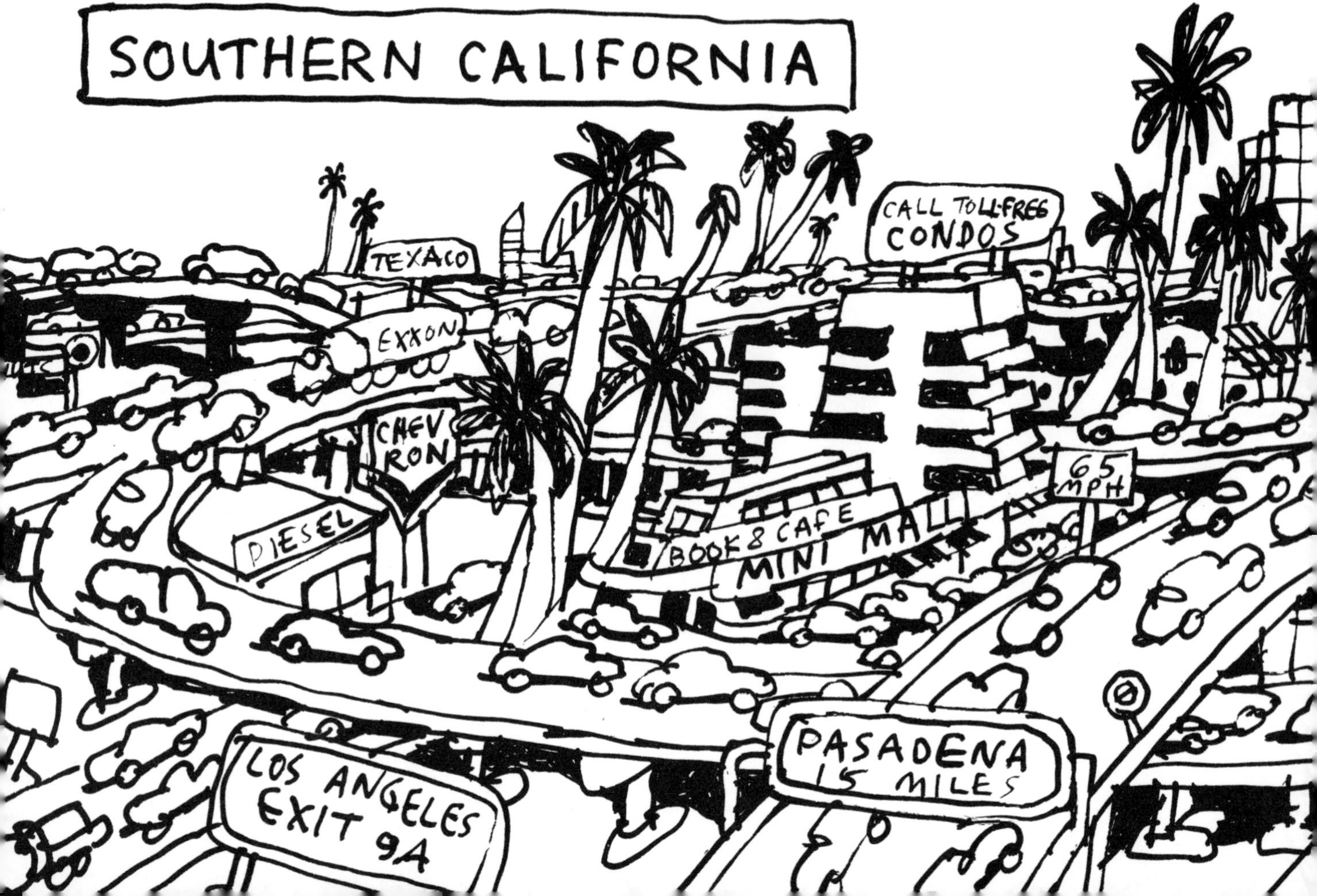
SOUTHERN CALIFORNIA
TEXACO
CALL TOLL-FREE
CONDOS
EXXON
CHEV
RON
DIESEL
65 MPH
BOOK & CAFE
MINI MA
LOS ANGELES
EXIT 9A
PASADENA
15 MILES

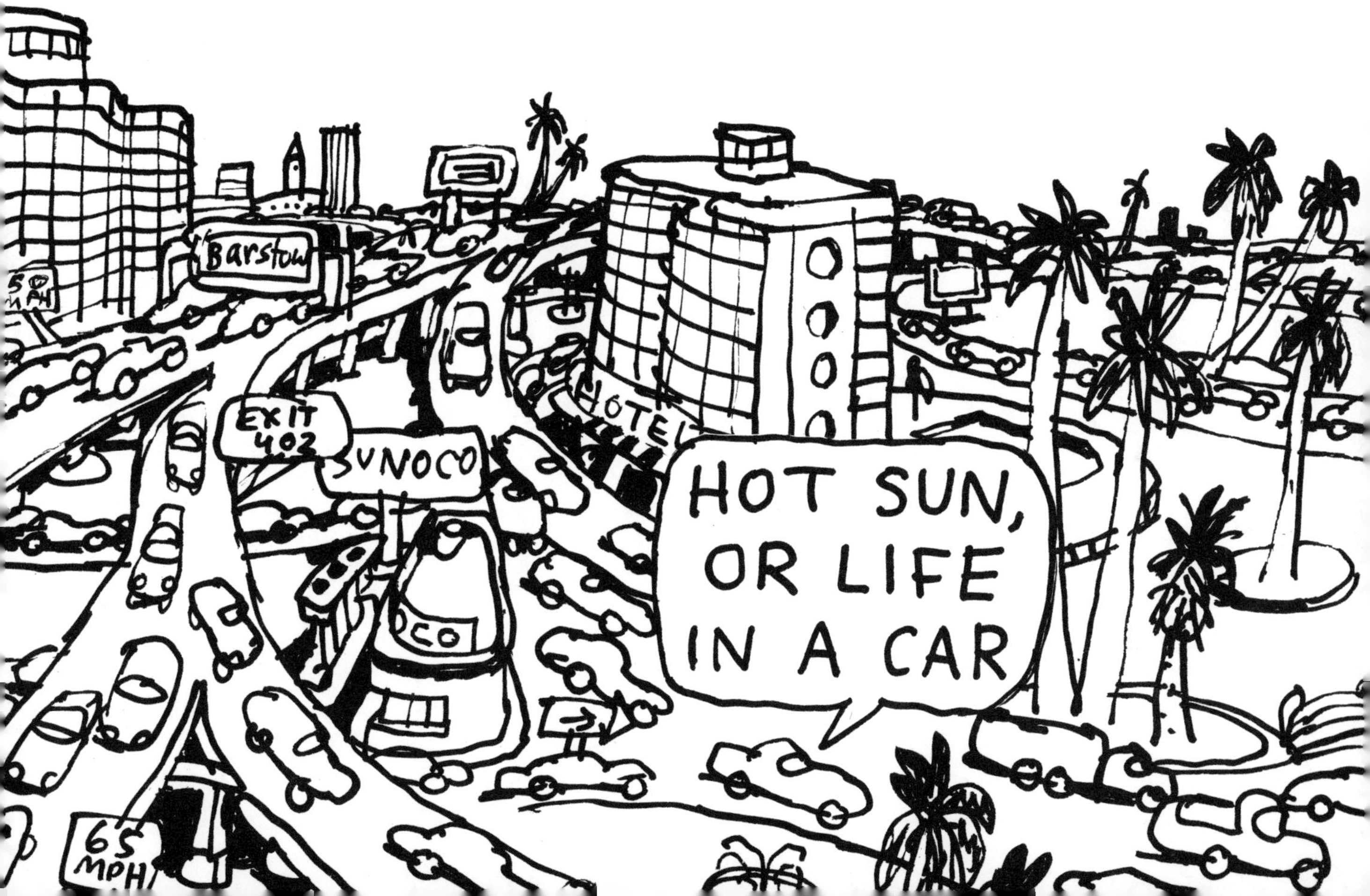
Barstow
50 MPH
EXIT 402
SUNOCO
HOTEL
OCO
65 MPH
HOT SUN, OR LIFE IN A CAR

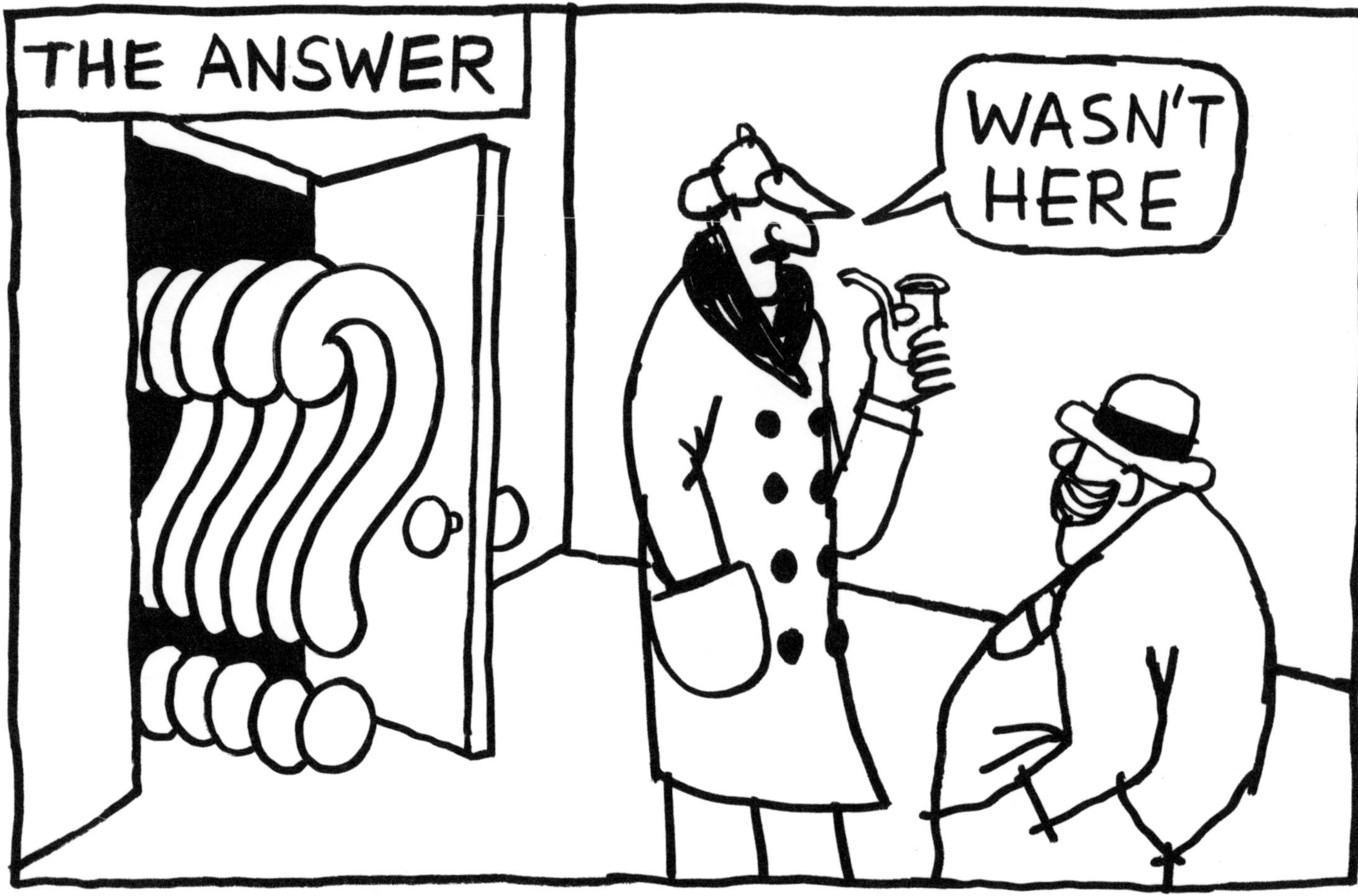
THE ANSWER
WASN'T HERE

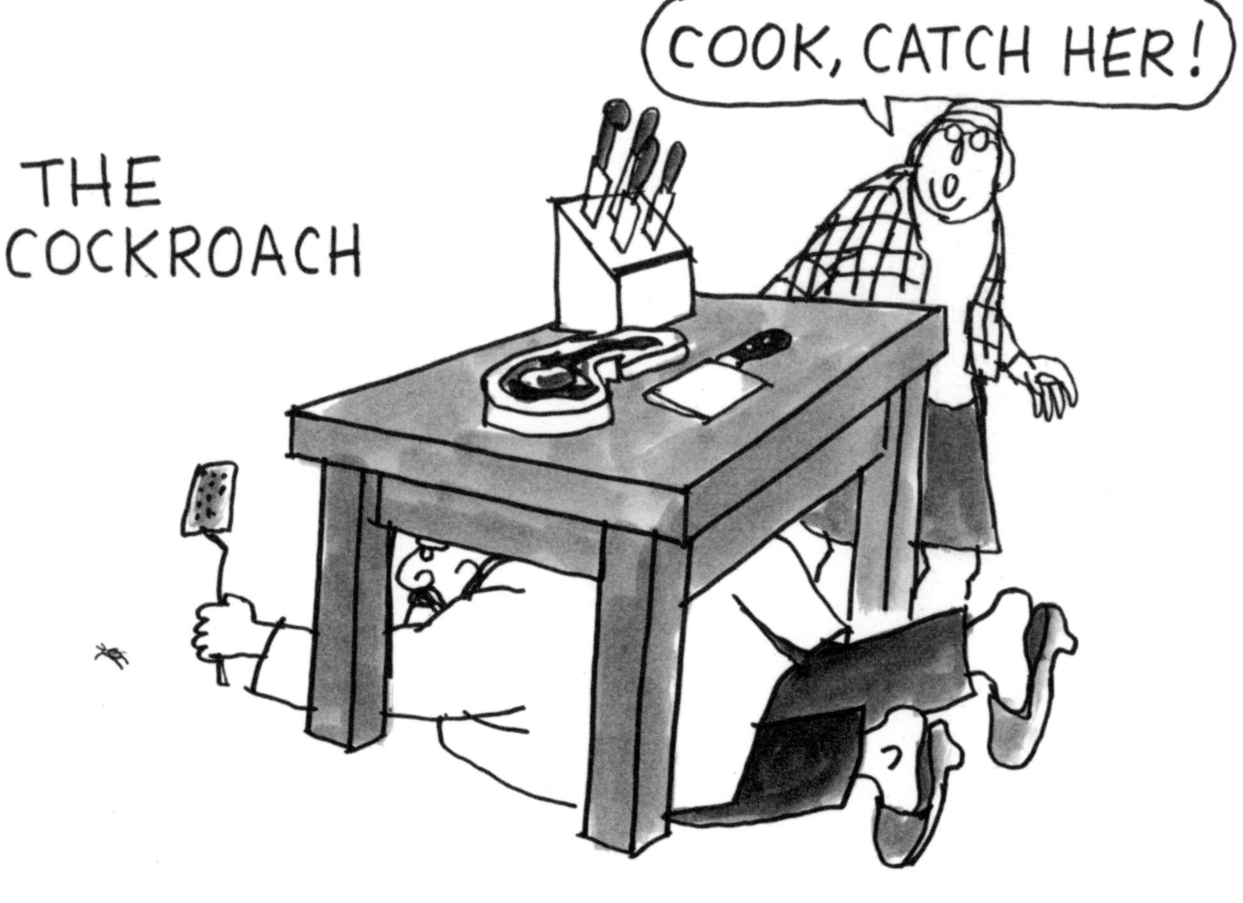
THE COCKROACH
COOK, CATCH HER!

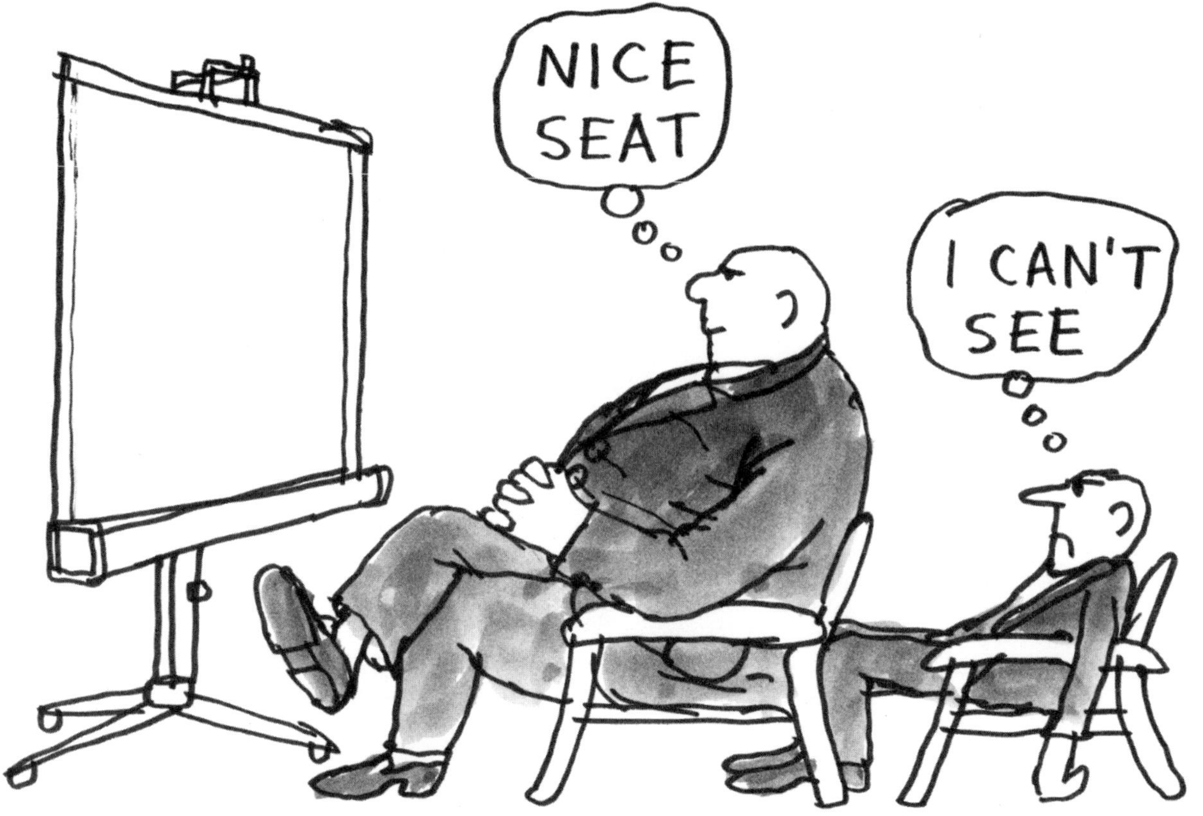
NICE SEAT
I CAN'T SEE

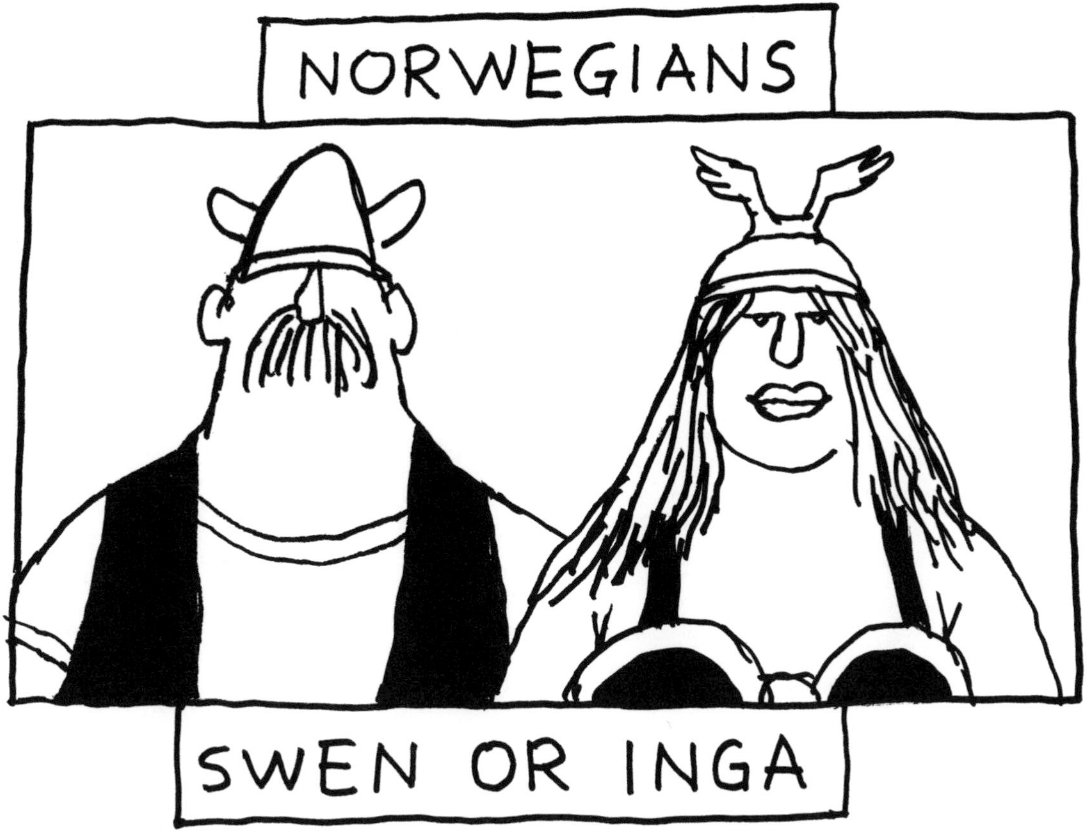
NORWEGIANS
SWEN OR INGA

ON ANY SCREEN

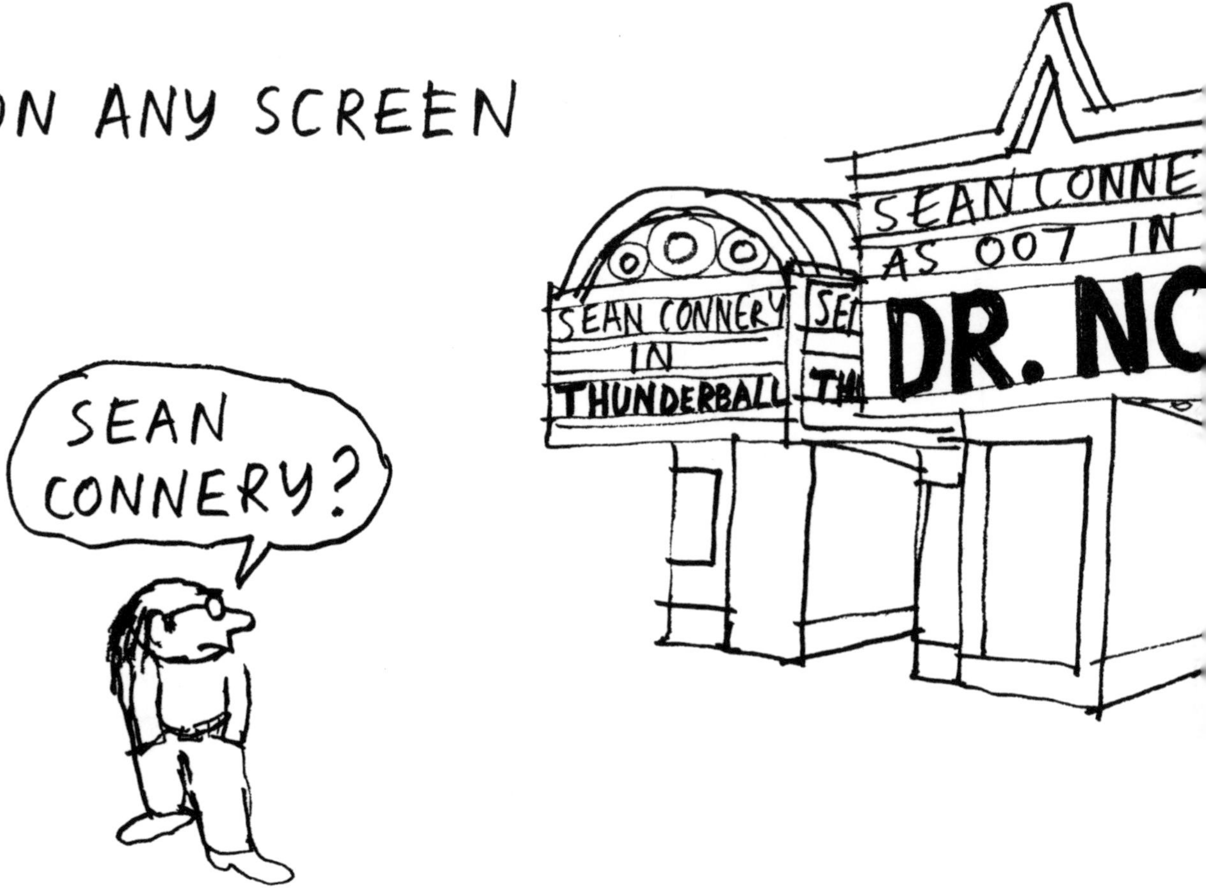
SEAN CONNERY?
SEAN CONNERY
IN
THUNDERBALL
SEAN CONNE
AS 007 IN
DR. N

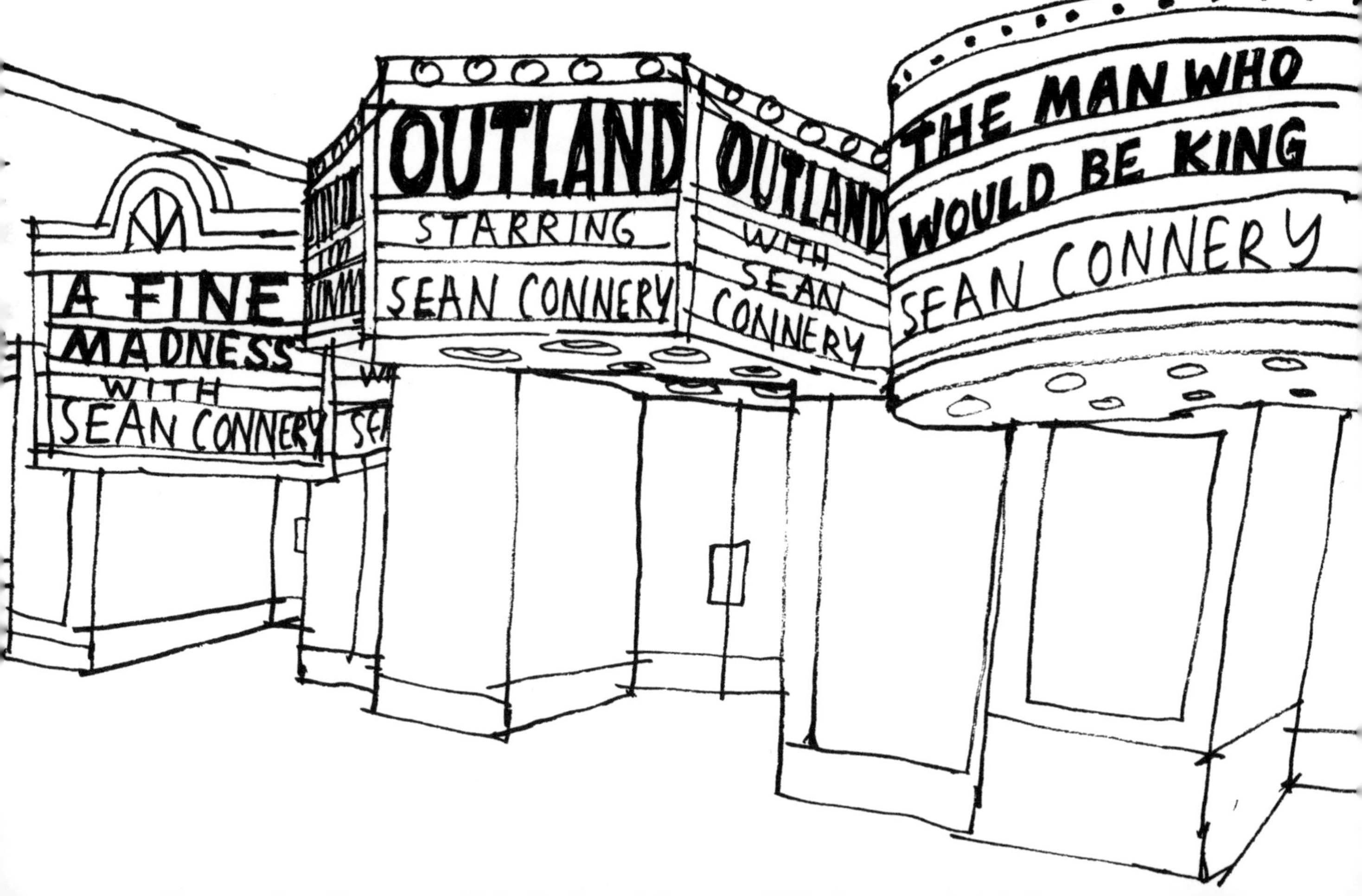
A FINE
MADNESS
WITH
SEAN CONNERY
OUTLAND
STARRING
SEAN CONNERY
OUTLAND
WITH
SEAN
CONNERY
THE MAN WHO
WOULD BE KING
SEAN CONNERY

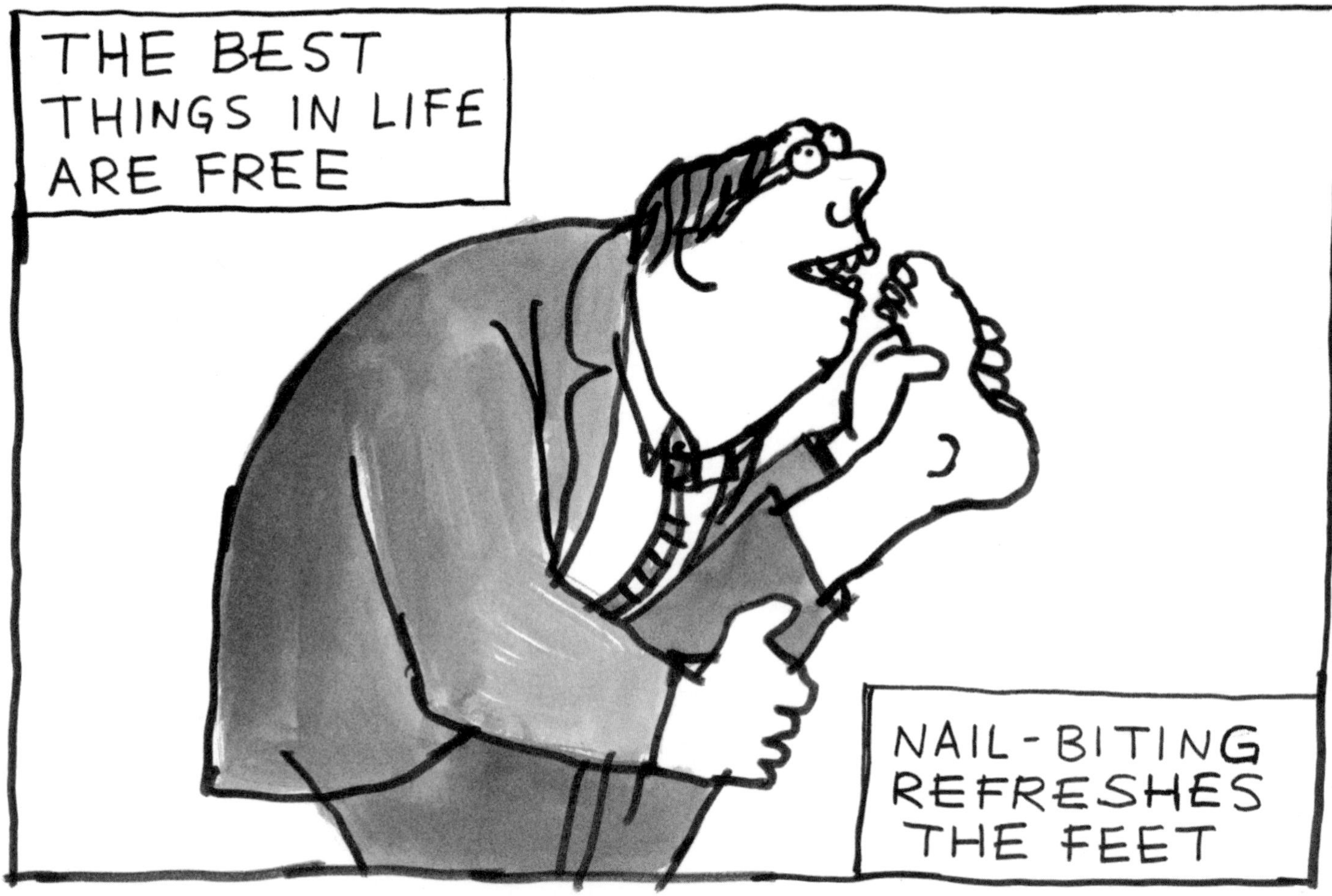
THE BEST THINGS IN LIFE ARE FREE
NAIL-BITING REFRESHES THE FEET

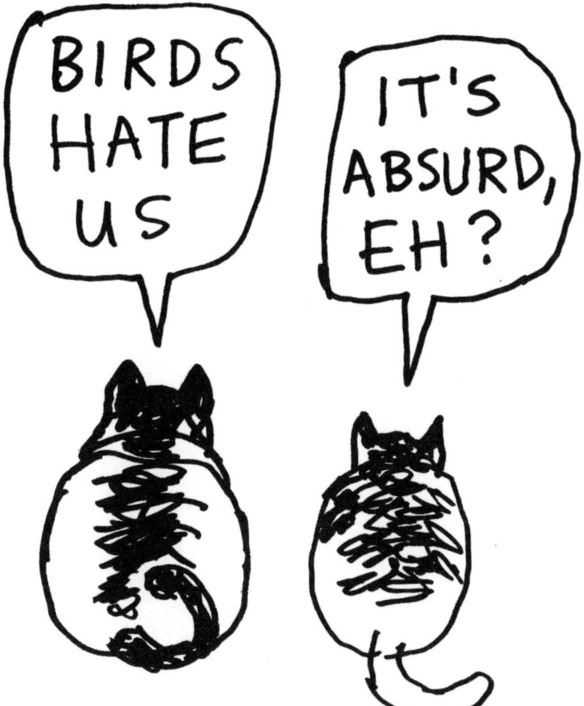
BIRDS HATE US
IT'S ABSURD, EH?

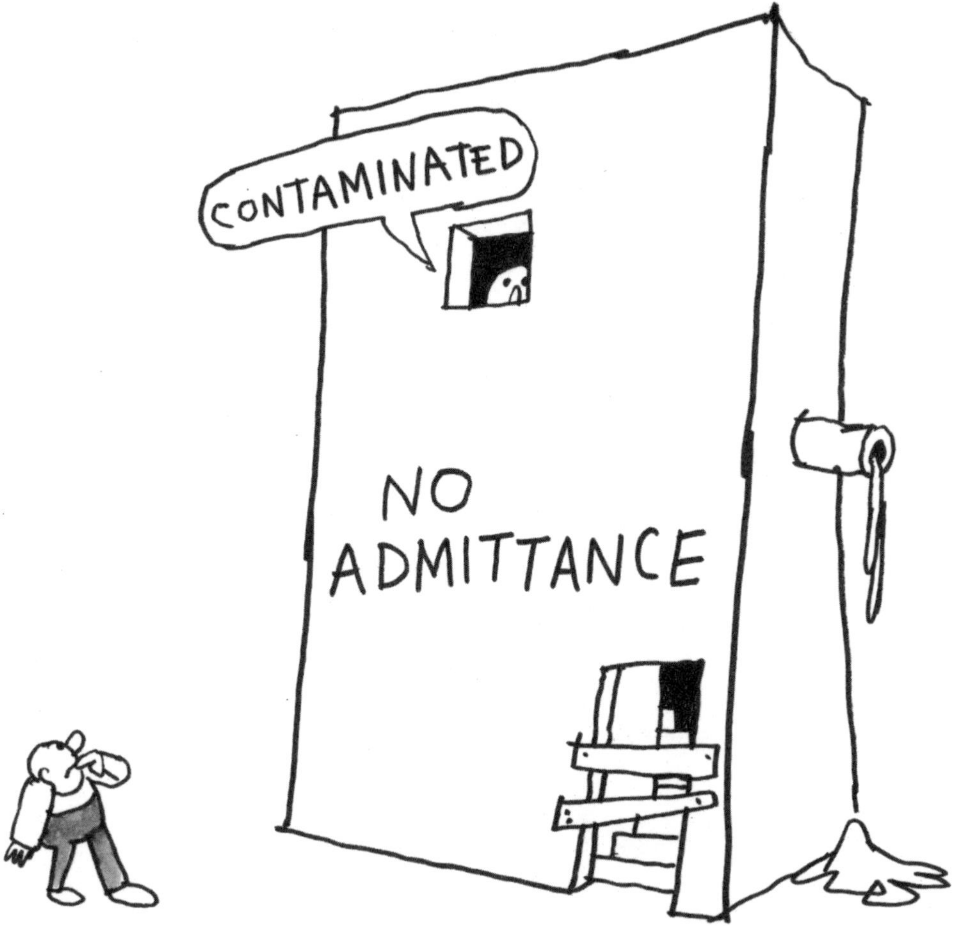
CONTAMINATED
NO ADMITTANCE

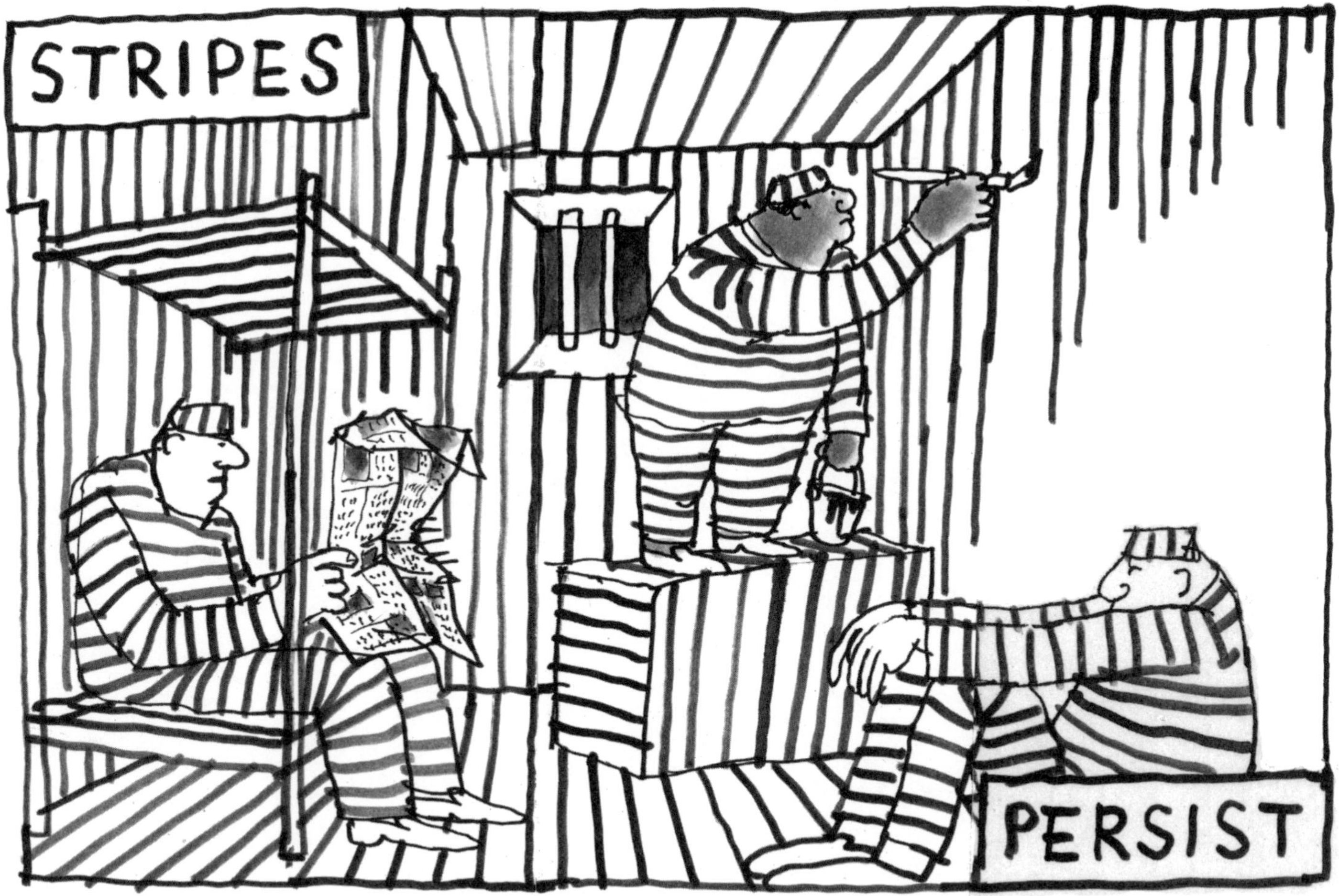
STRIPES
PERSIST

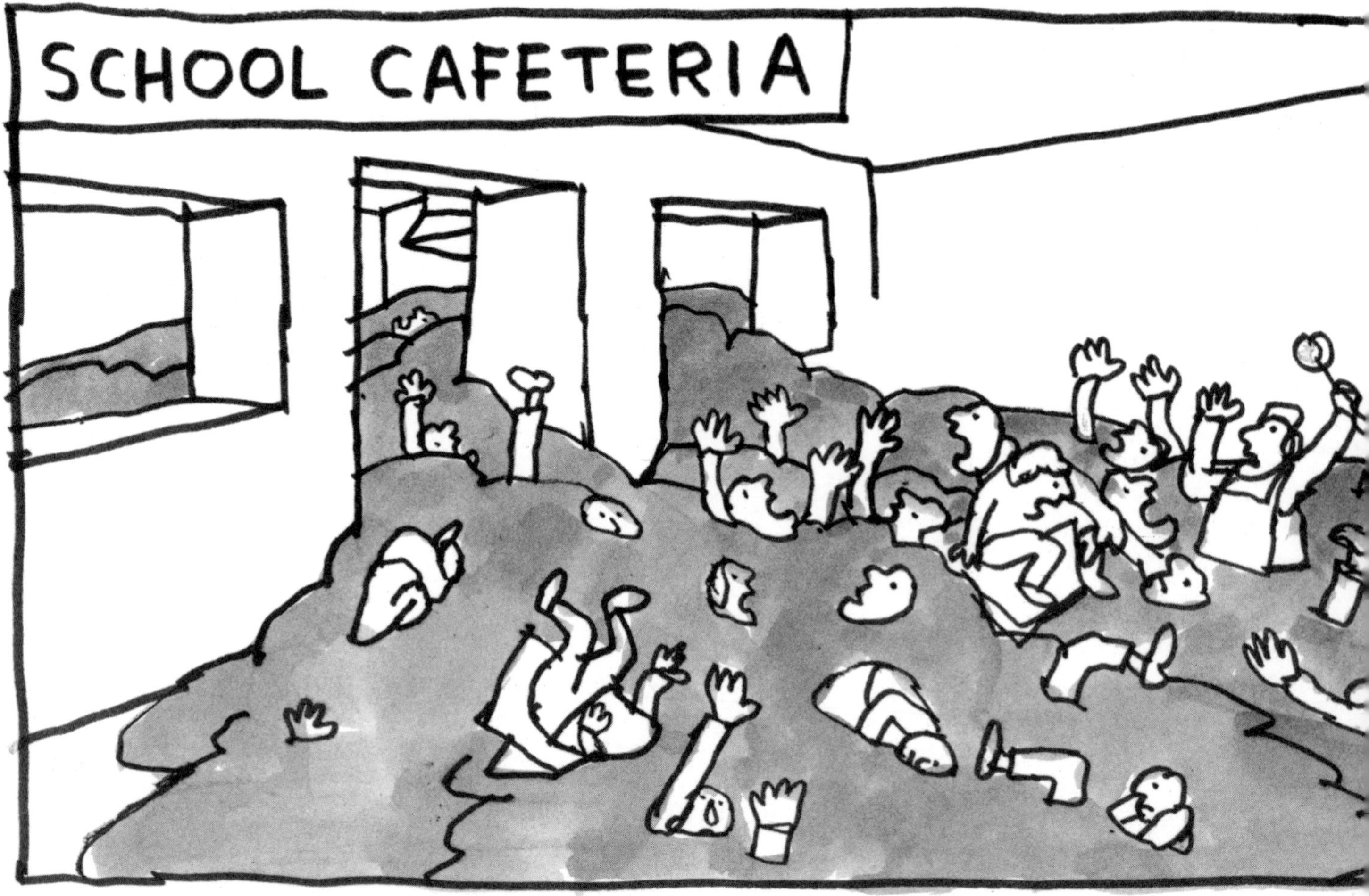
SCHOOL CAFETERIA

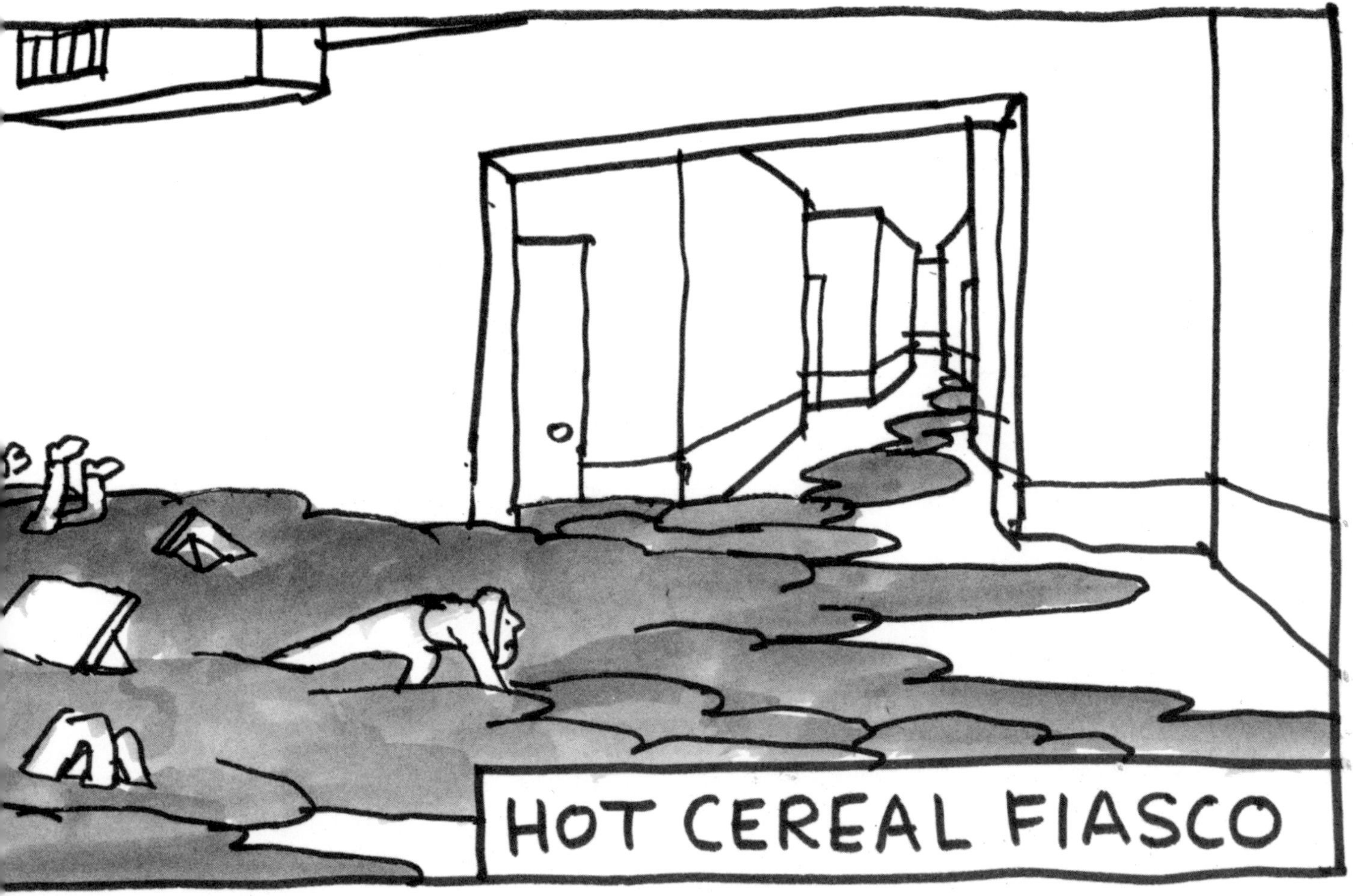
HOT CEREAL FIASCO

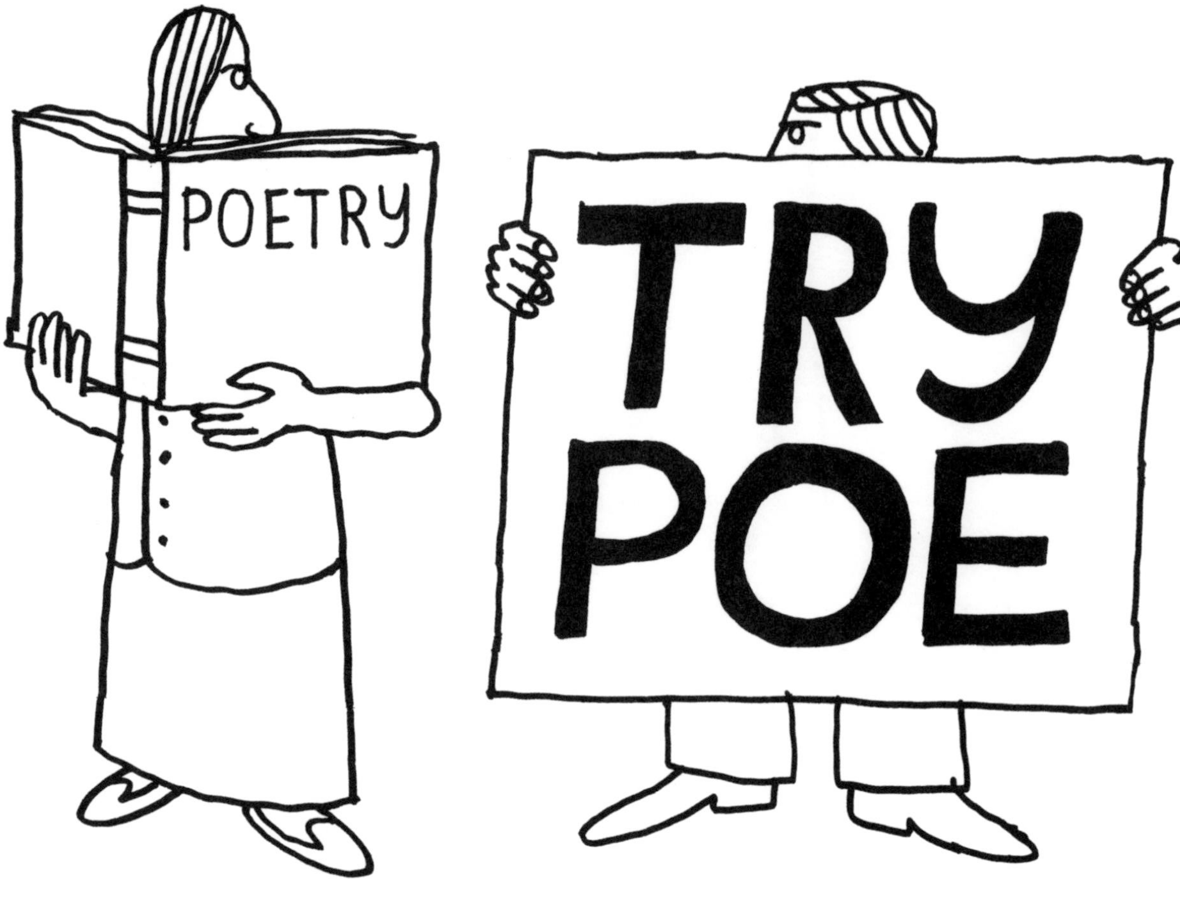
POETRY
TRY
POE

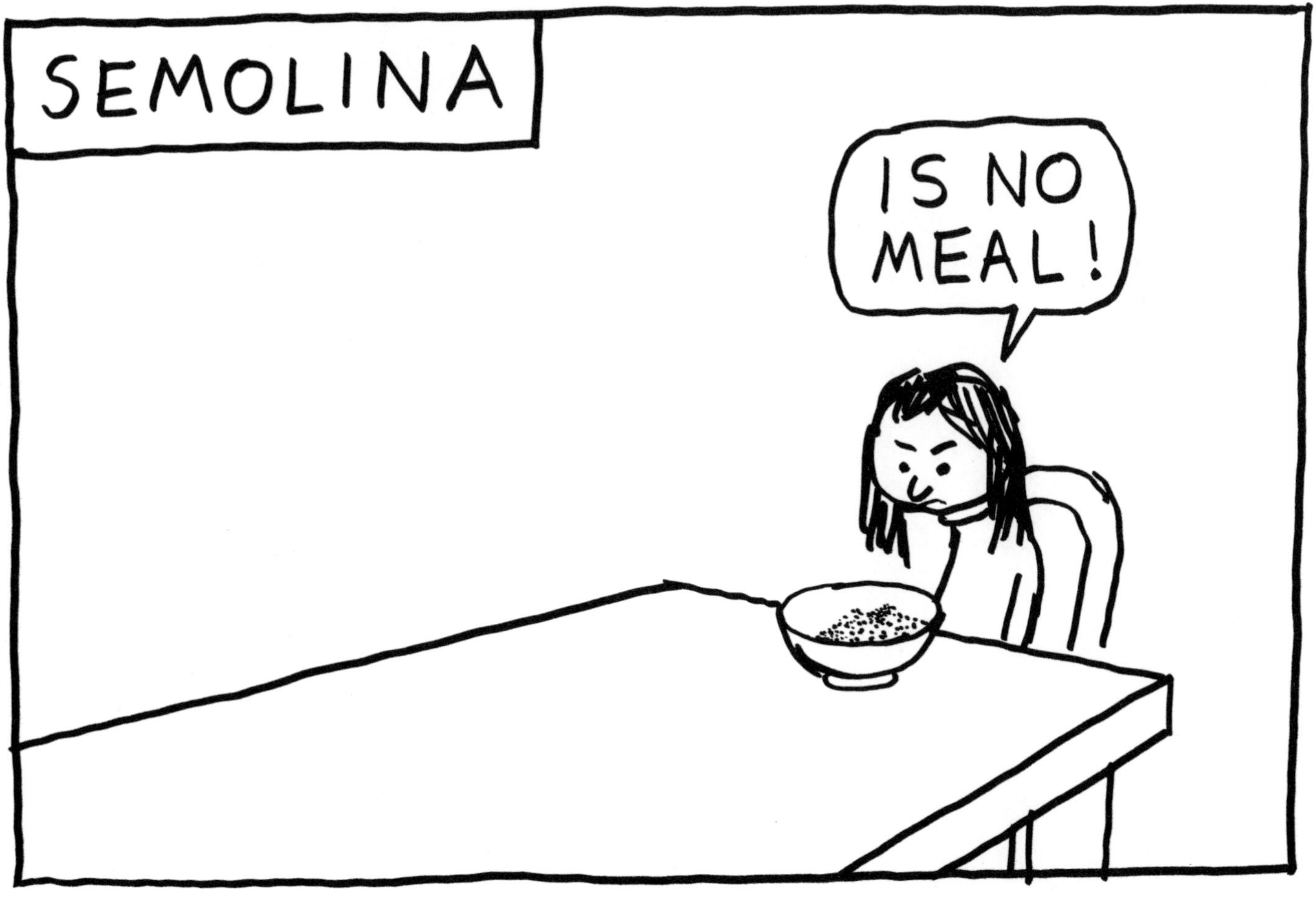
SEMOLINA
IS NO MEAL!

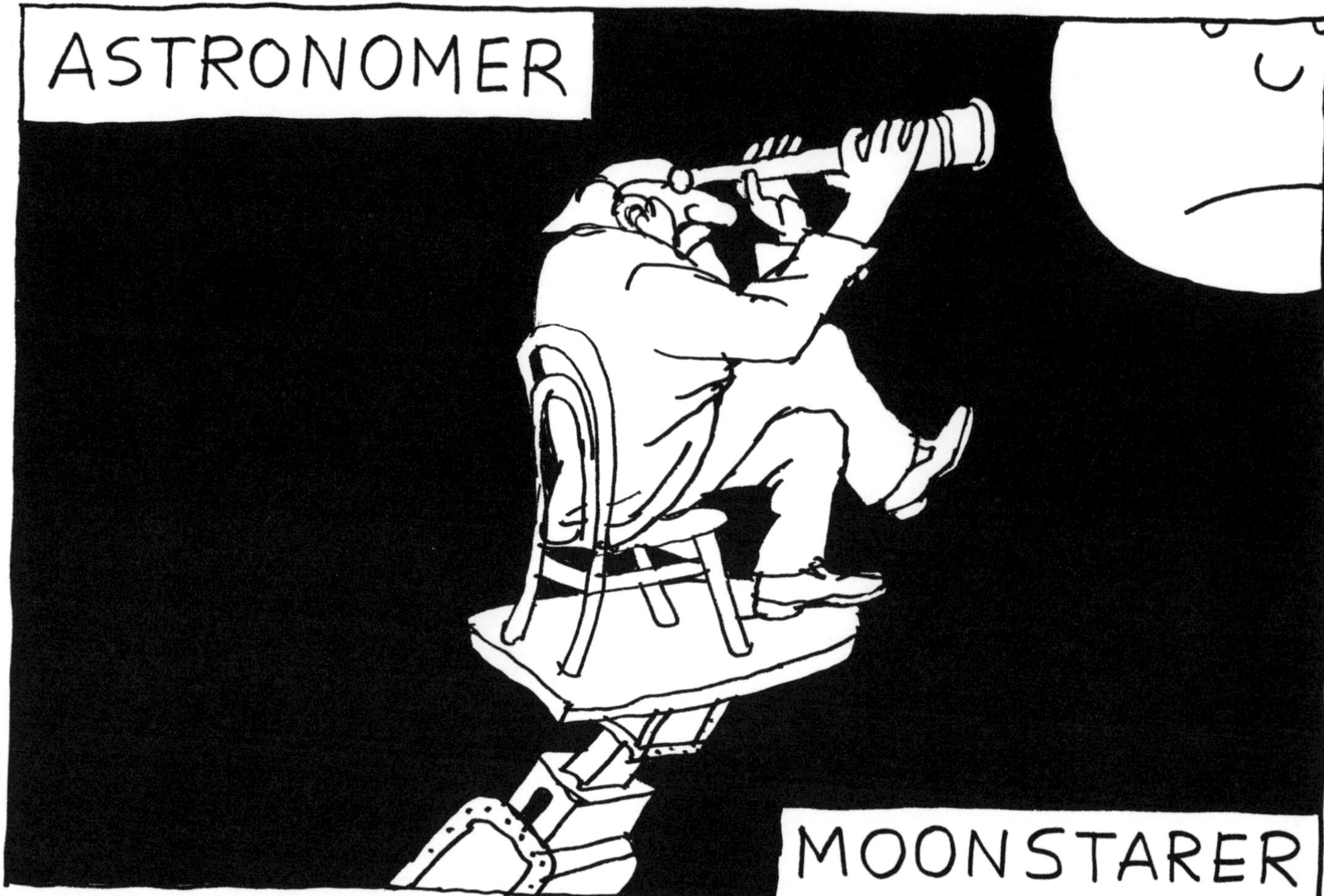
ASTRONOMER
MOONSTARER

HARPS

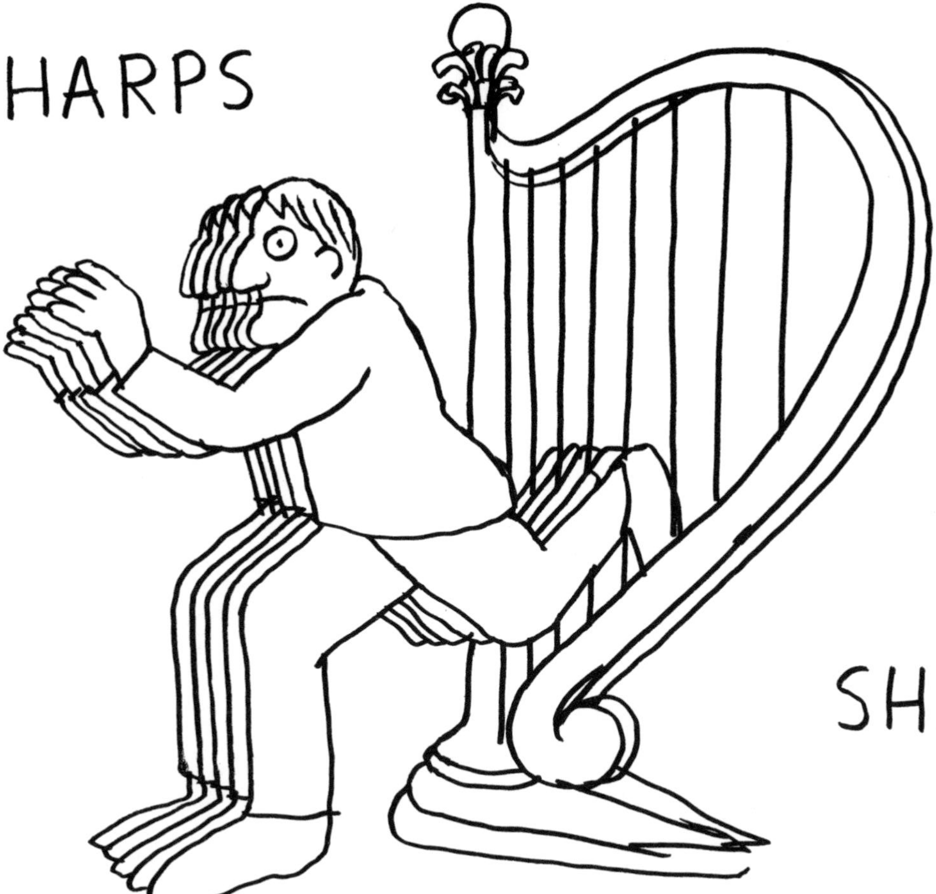

SHARP

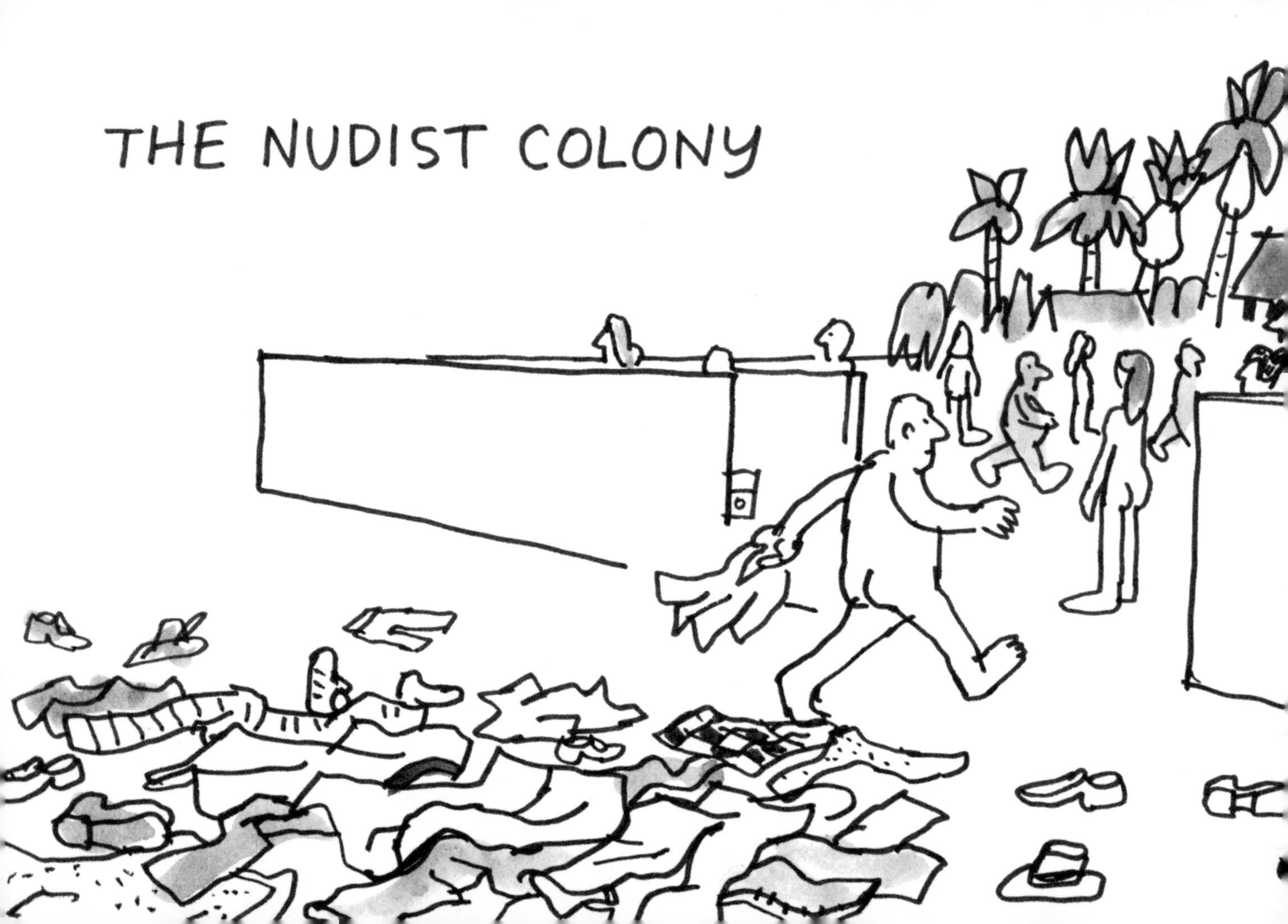
THE NUDIST COLONY

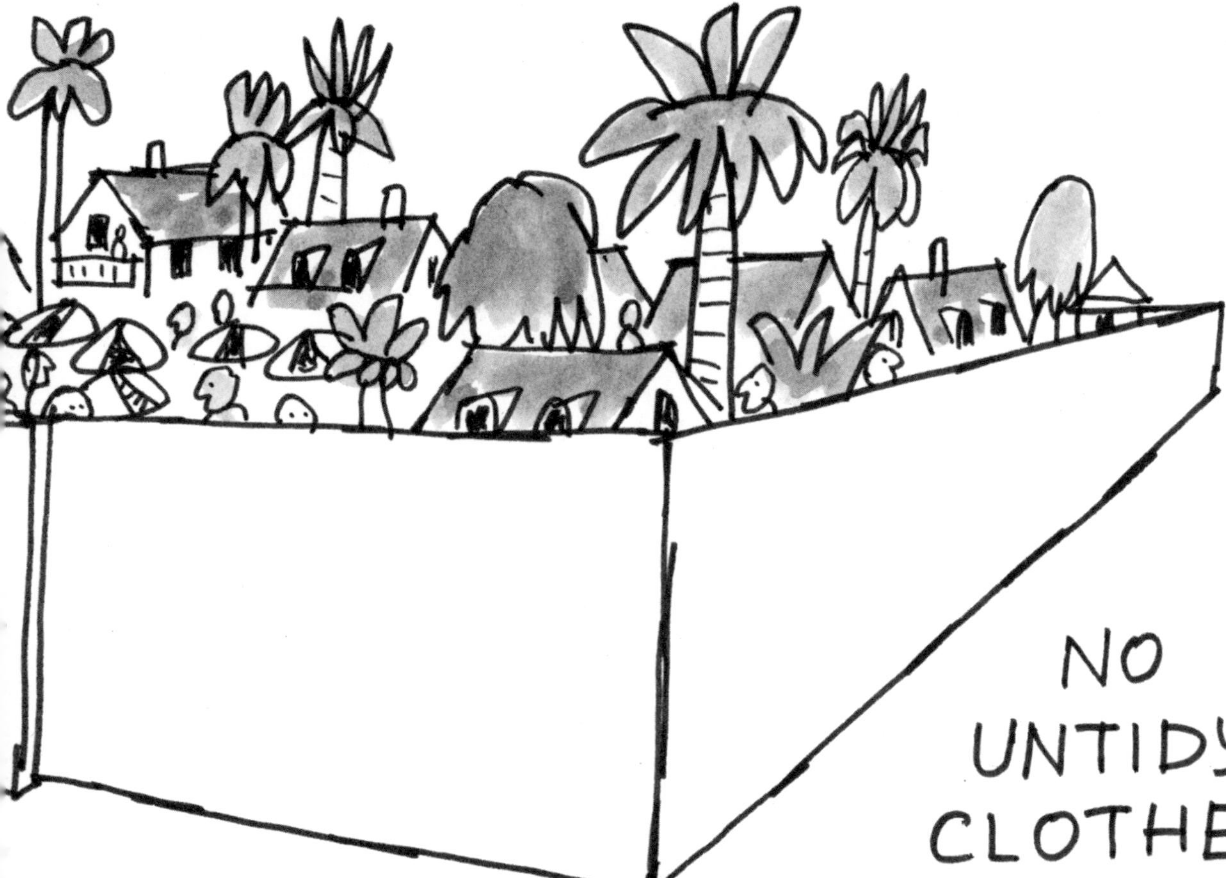

NO
UNTIDY
CLOTHES

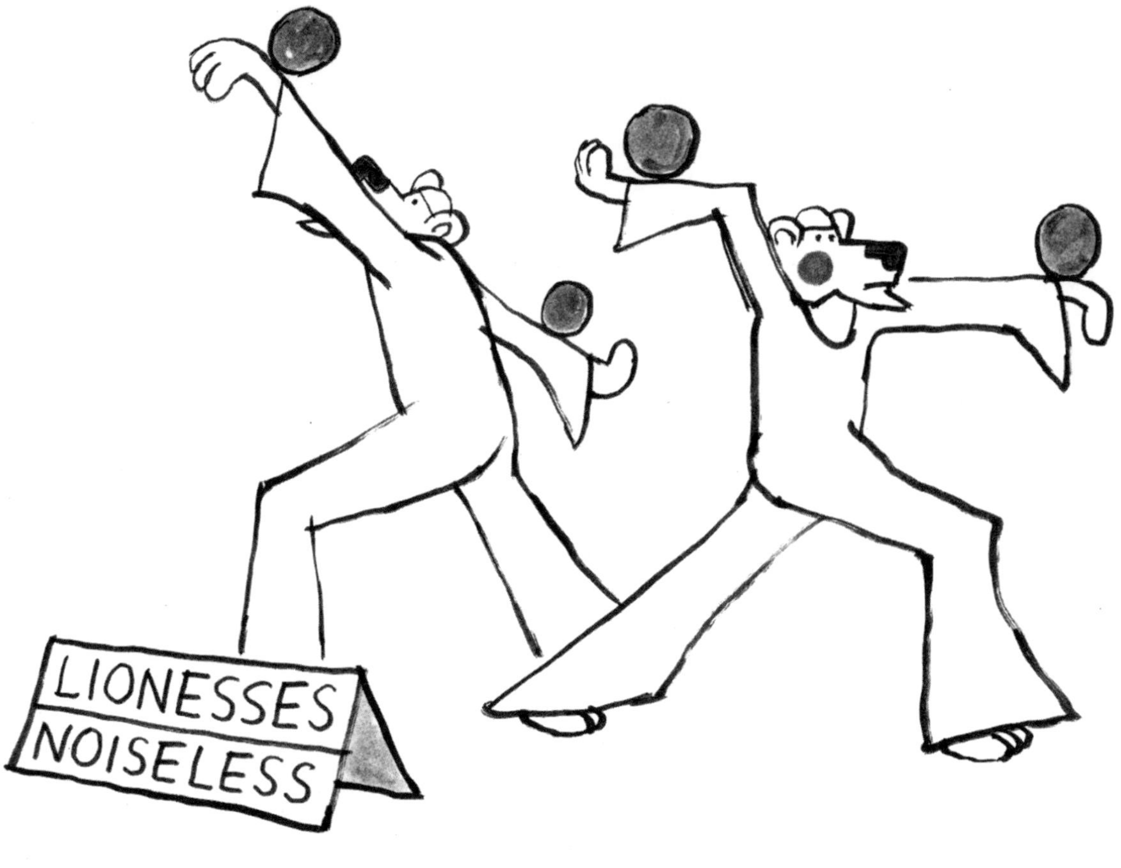
LIONESSES
NOISELESS

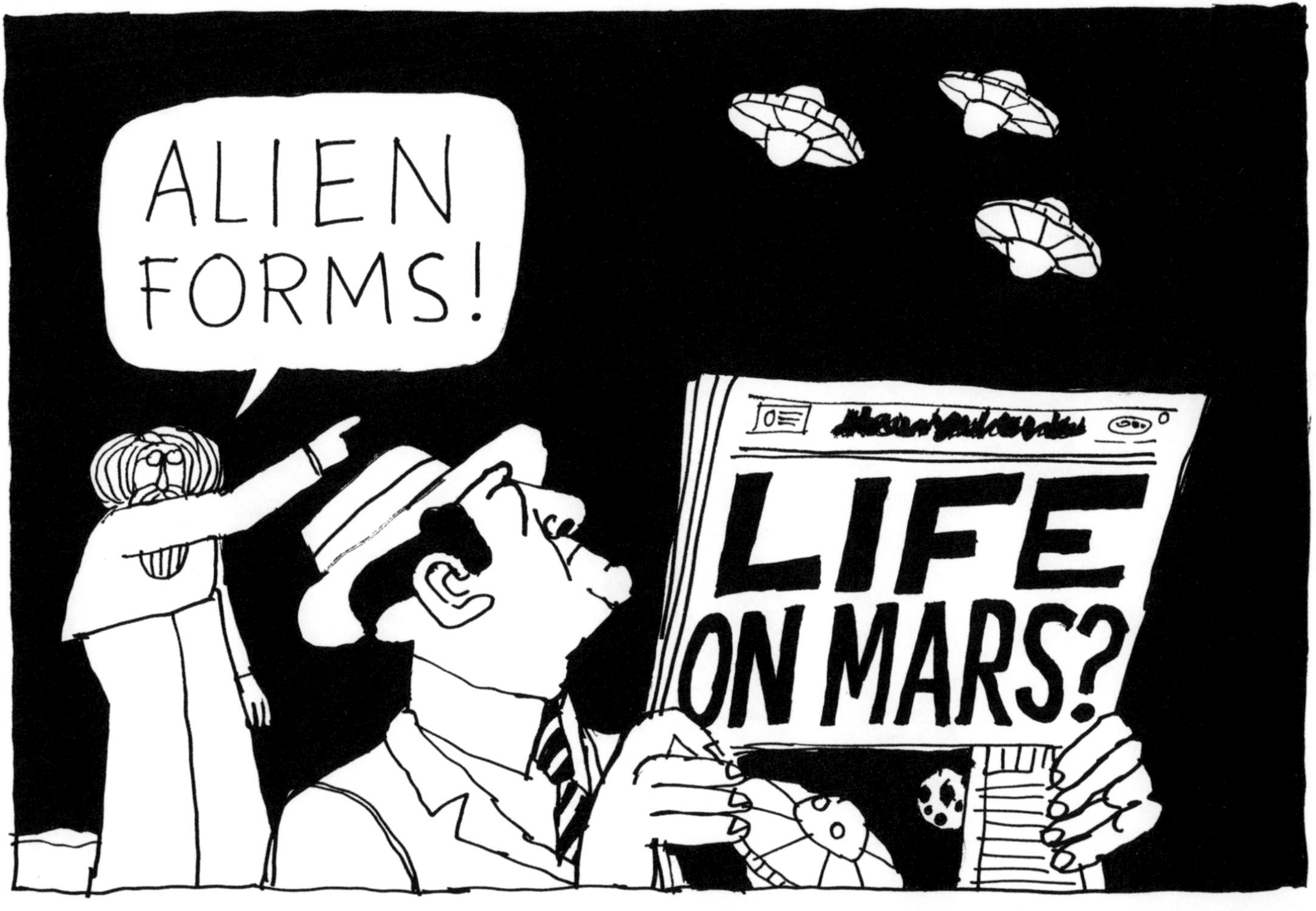
ALIEN FORMS!
LIFE ON MARS?

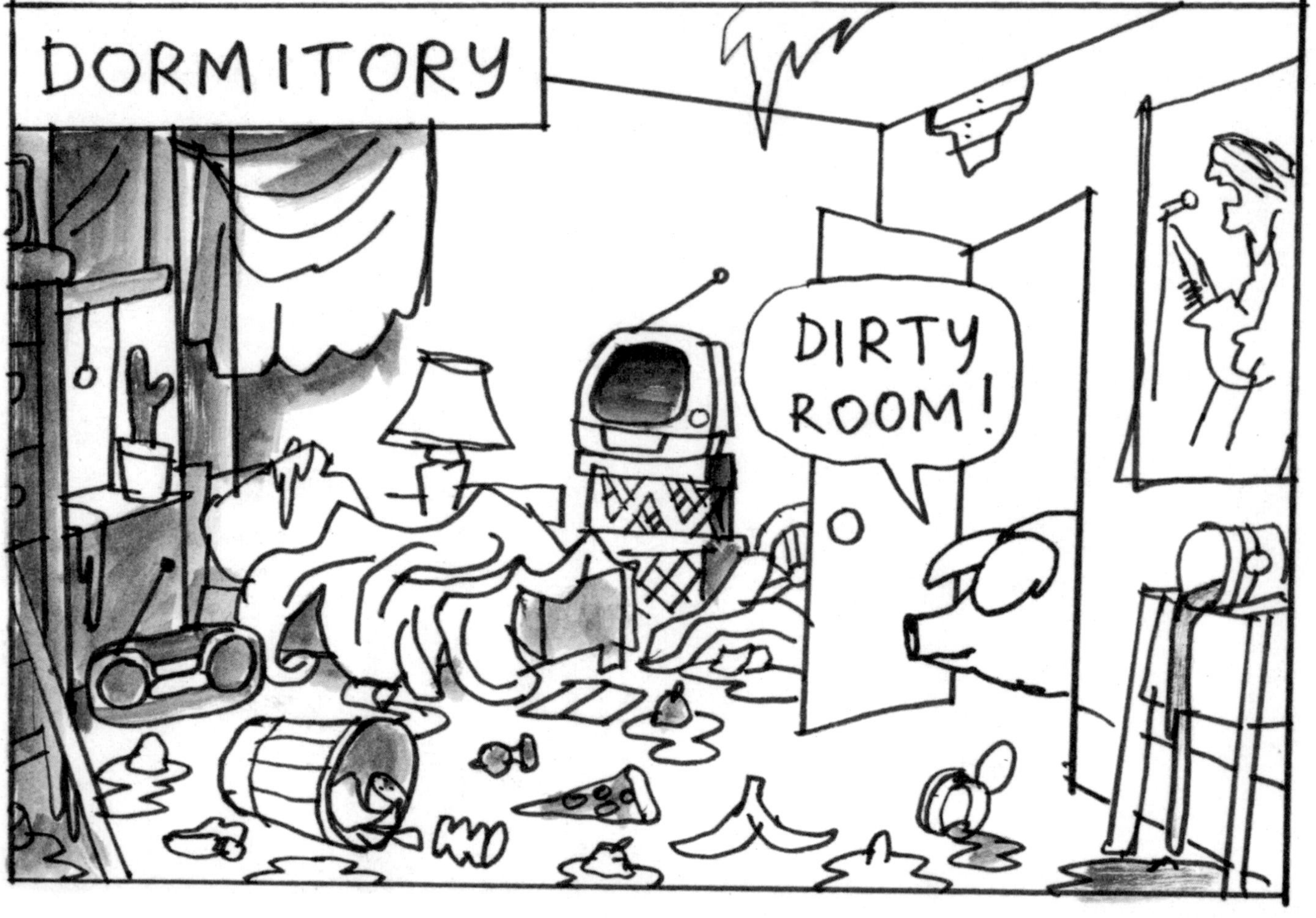
DORMITORY
DIRTY ROOM!

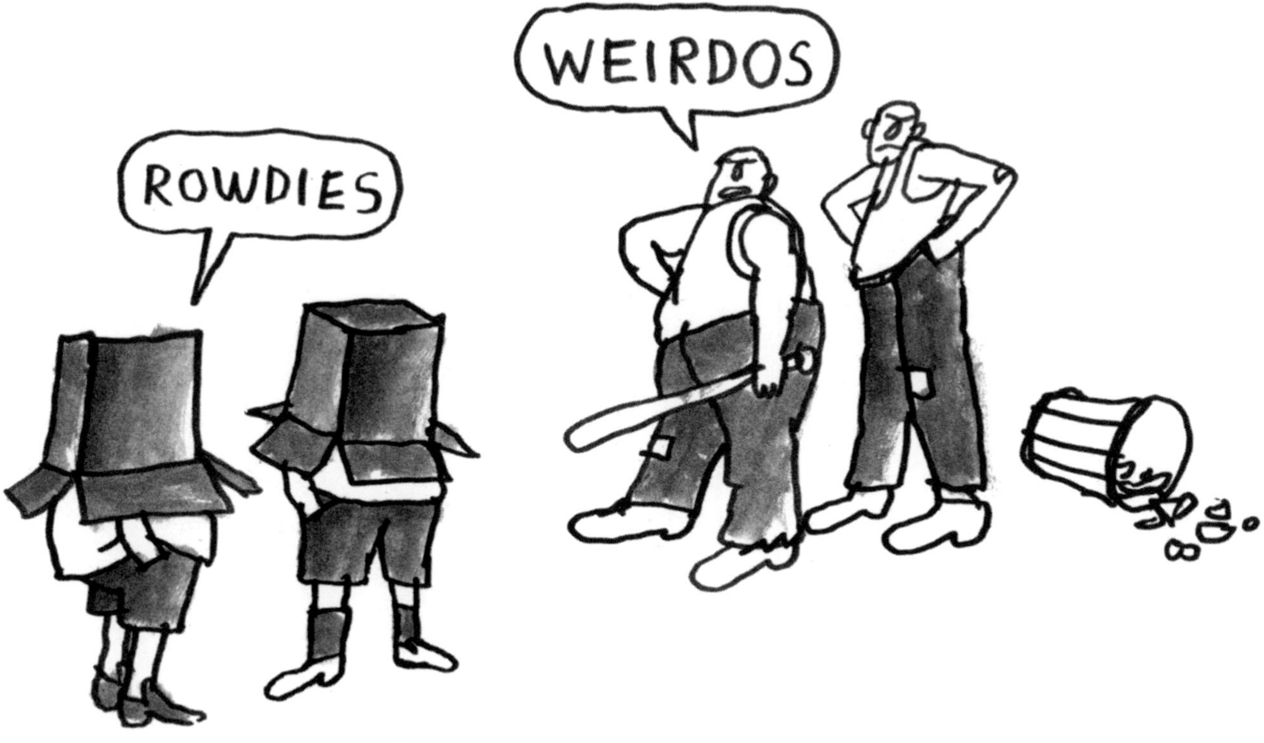
ROWDIES
WEIRDOS

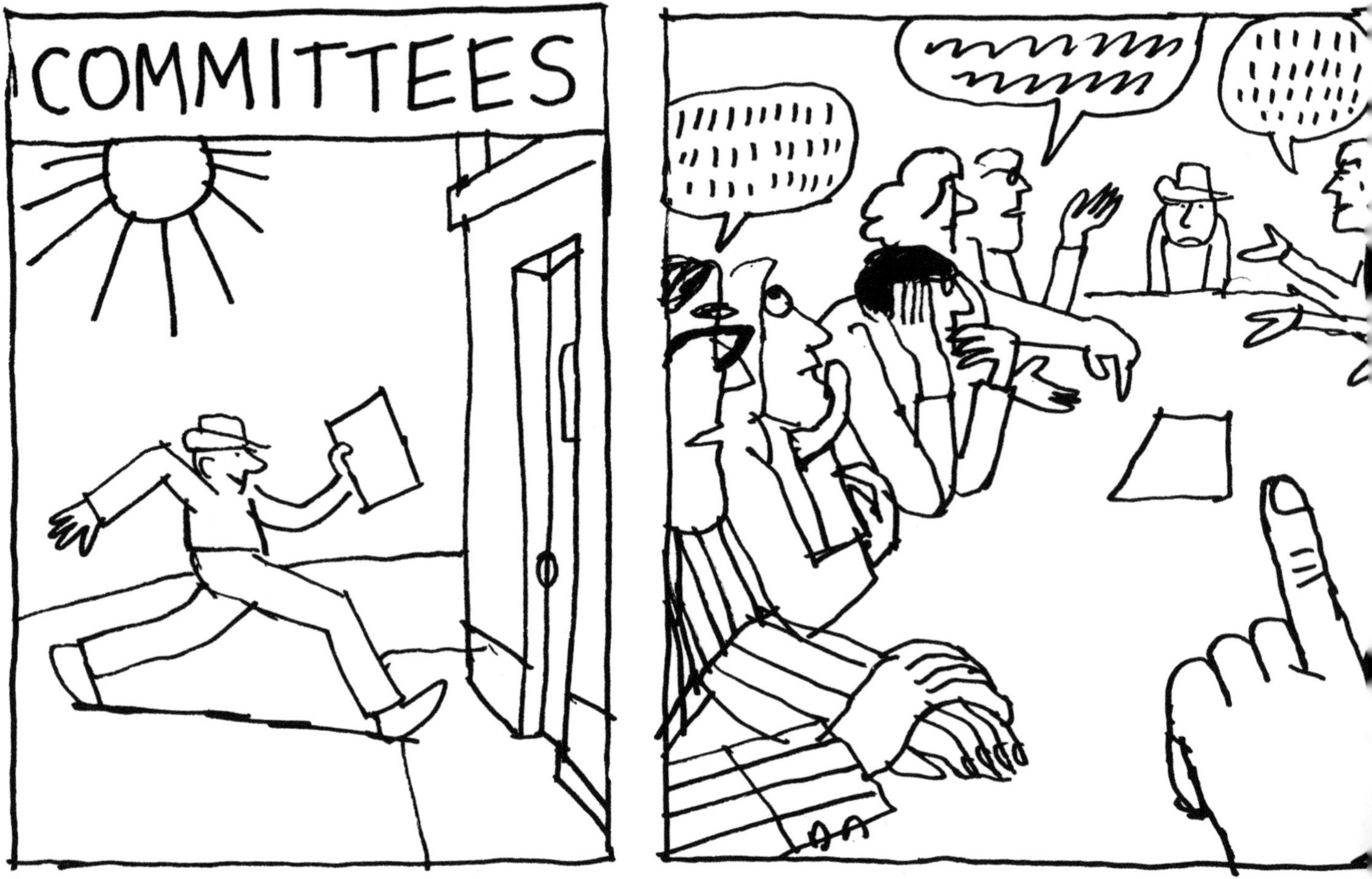
COMMITTEES

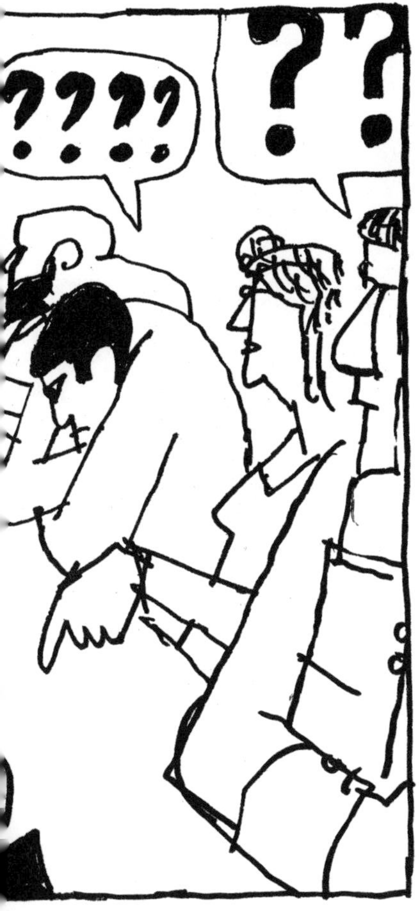
????
??

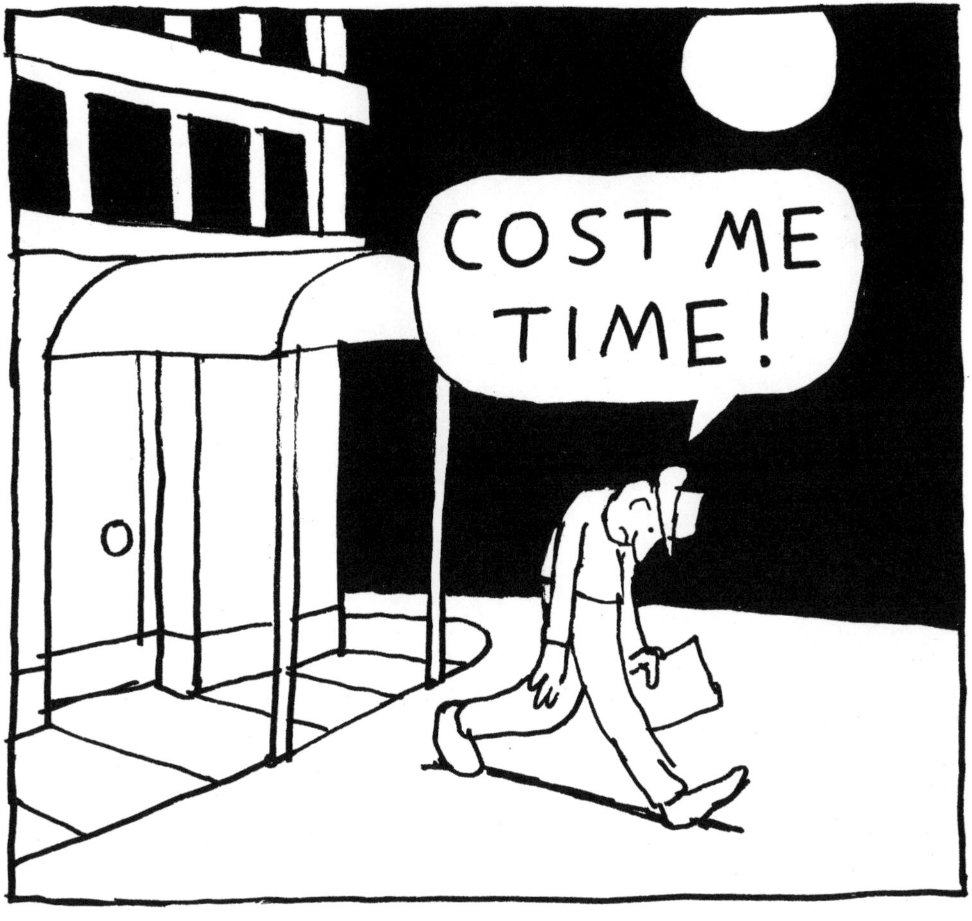
COST ME TIME!

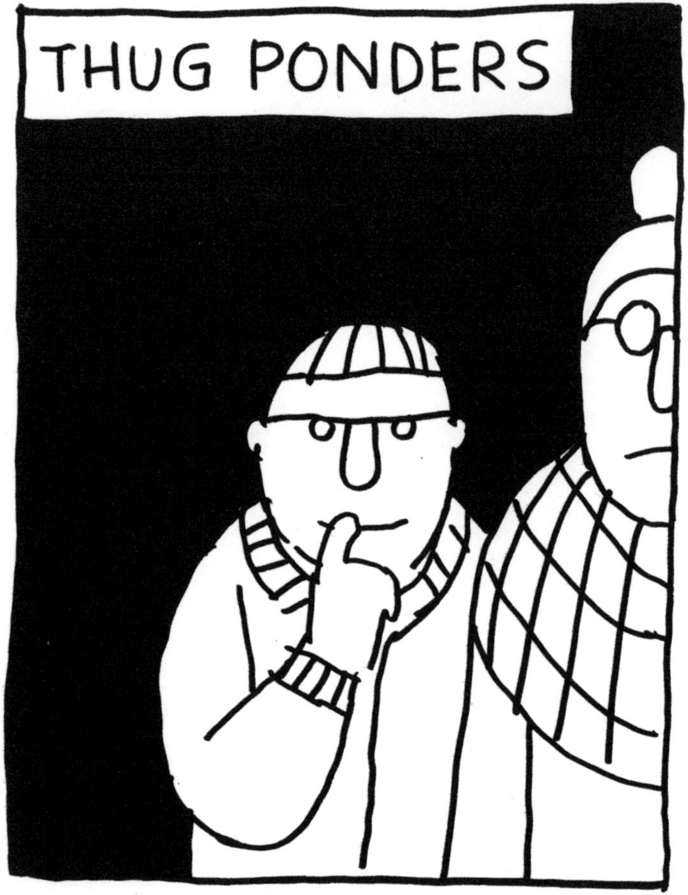
THUG PONDERS

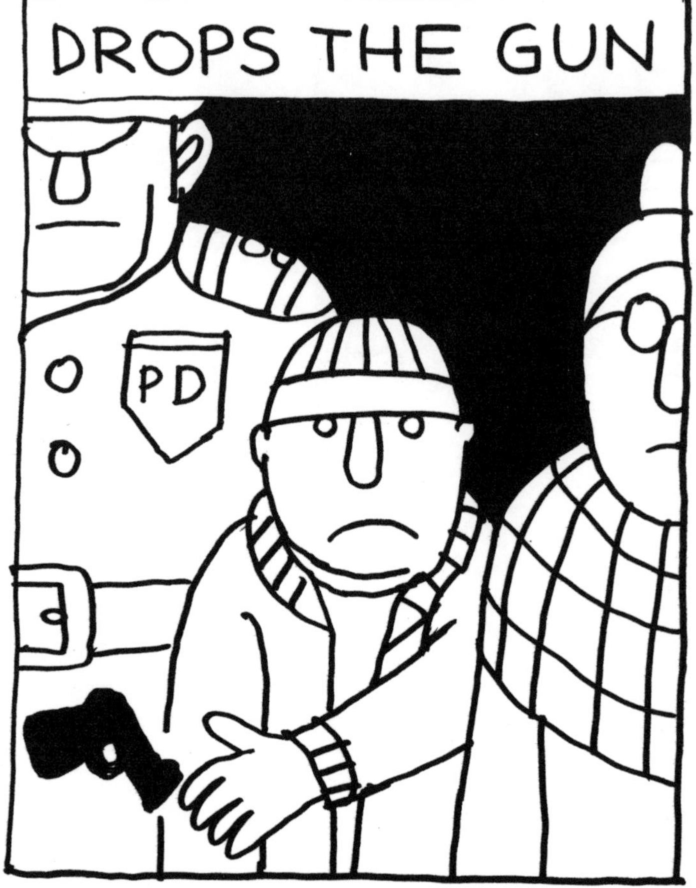
DROPS THE GUN
PD

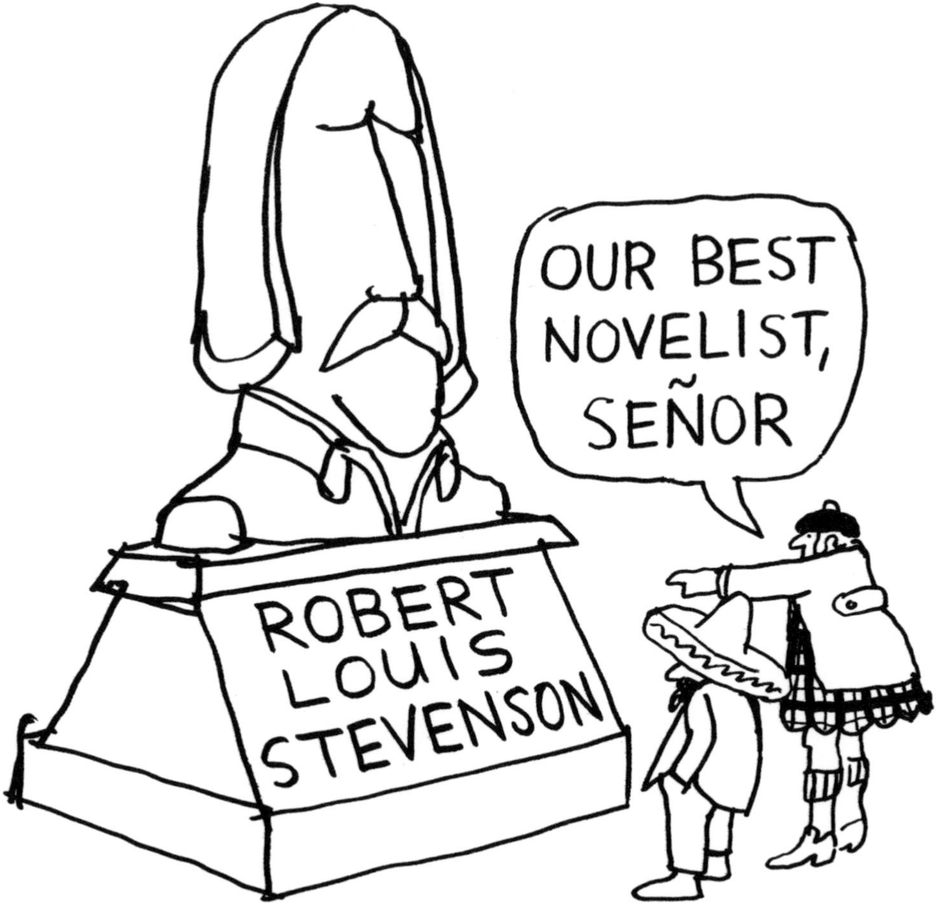
ROBERT LOUIS STEVENSON
OUR BEST NOVELIST, SEÑOR

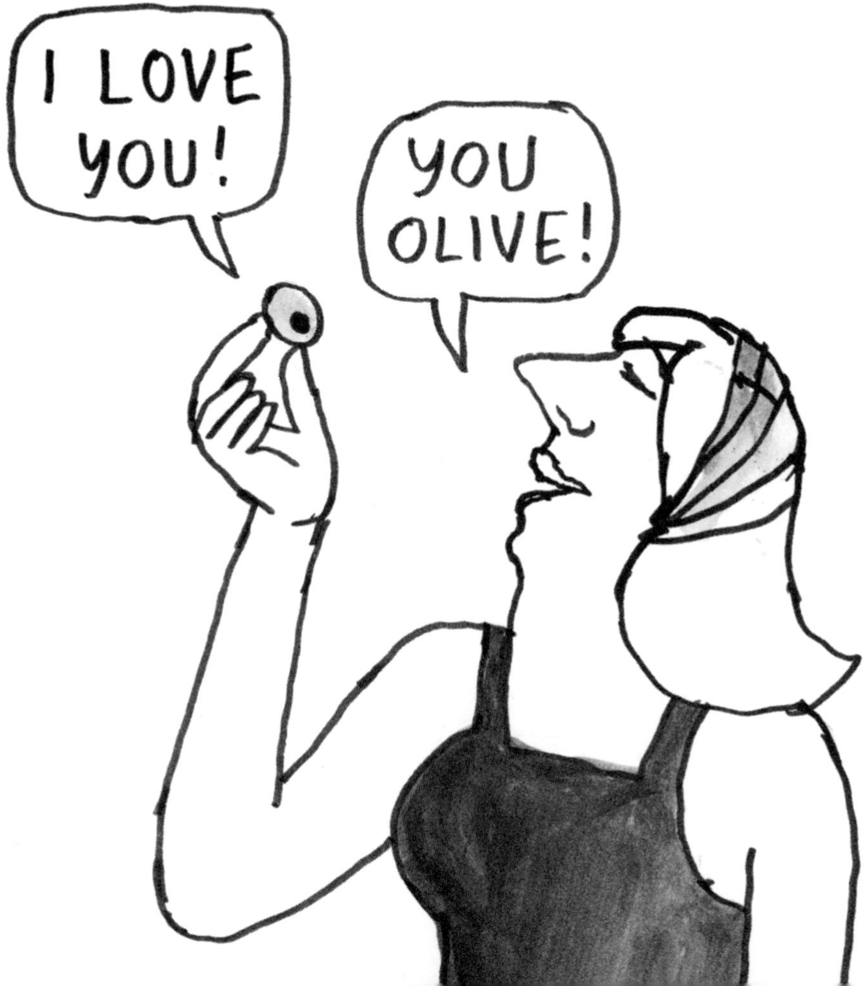
I LOVE YOU!
YOU OLIVE!

THE PIANO BENCH

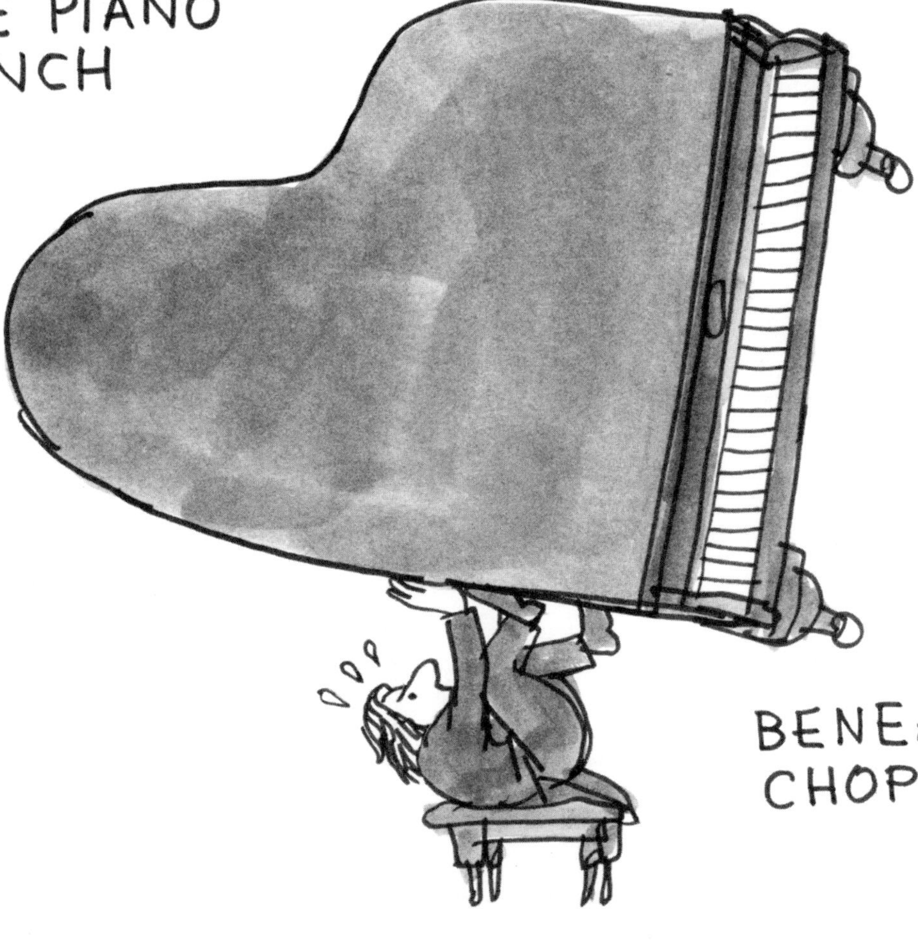

BENEATH CHOPIN

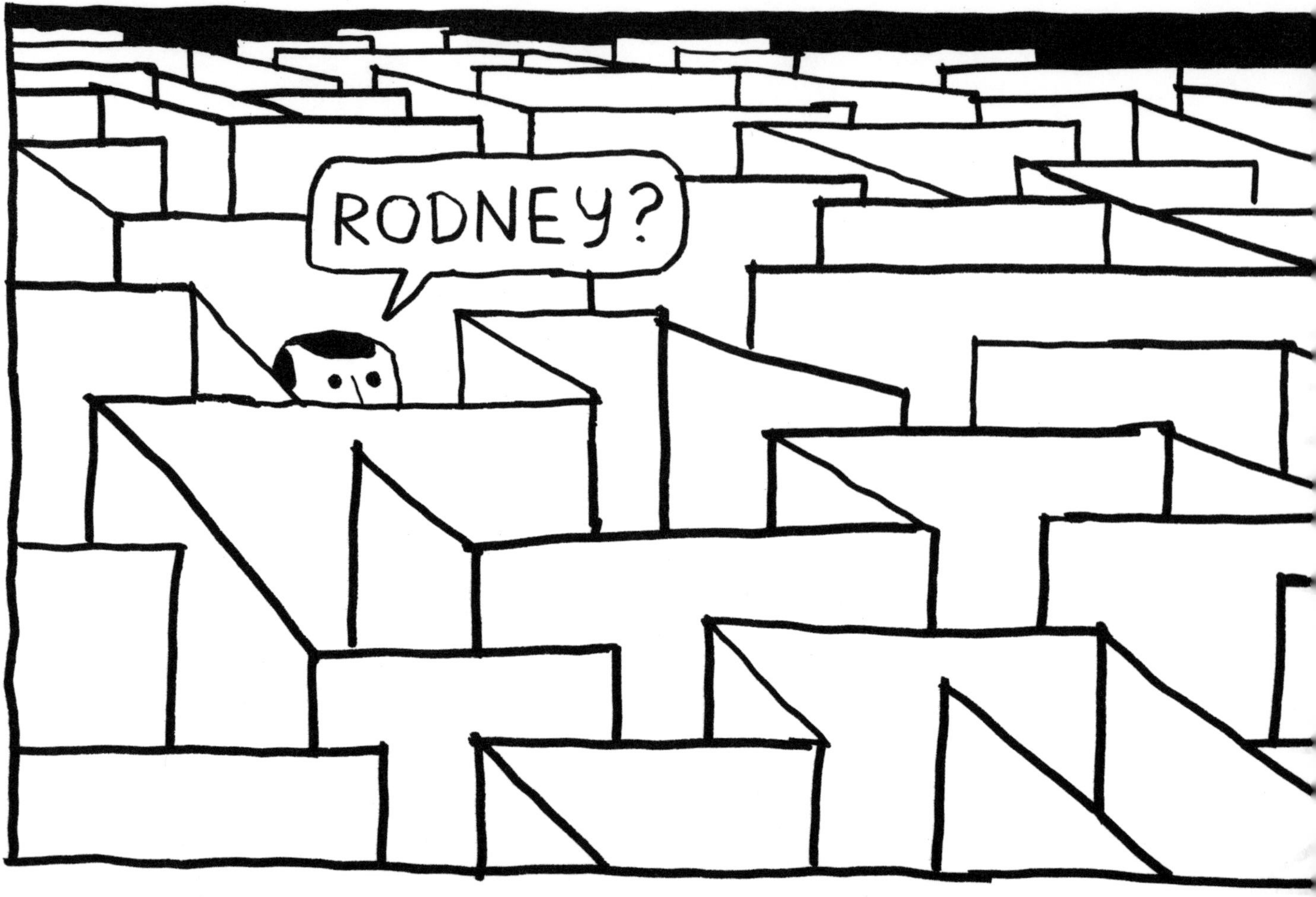
RODNEY?

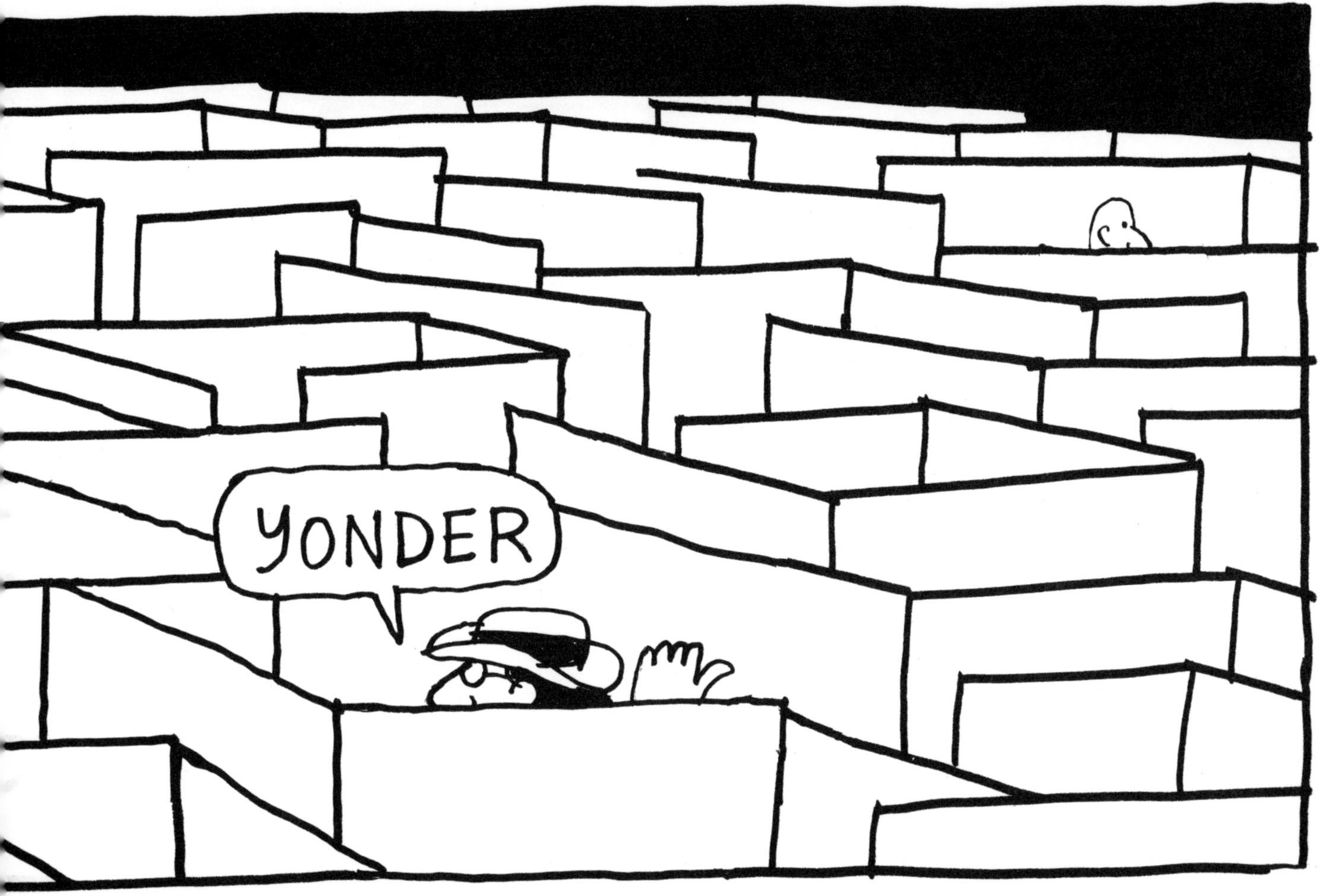
YONDER

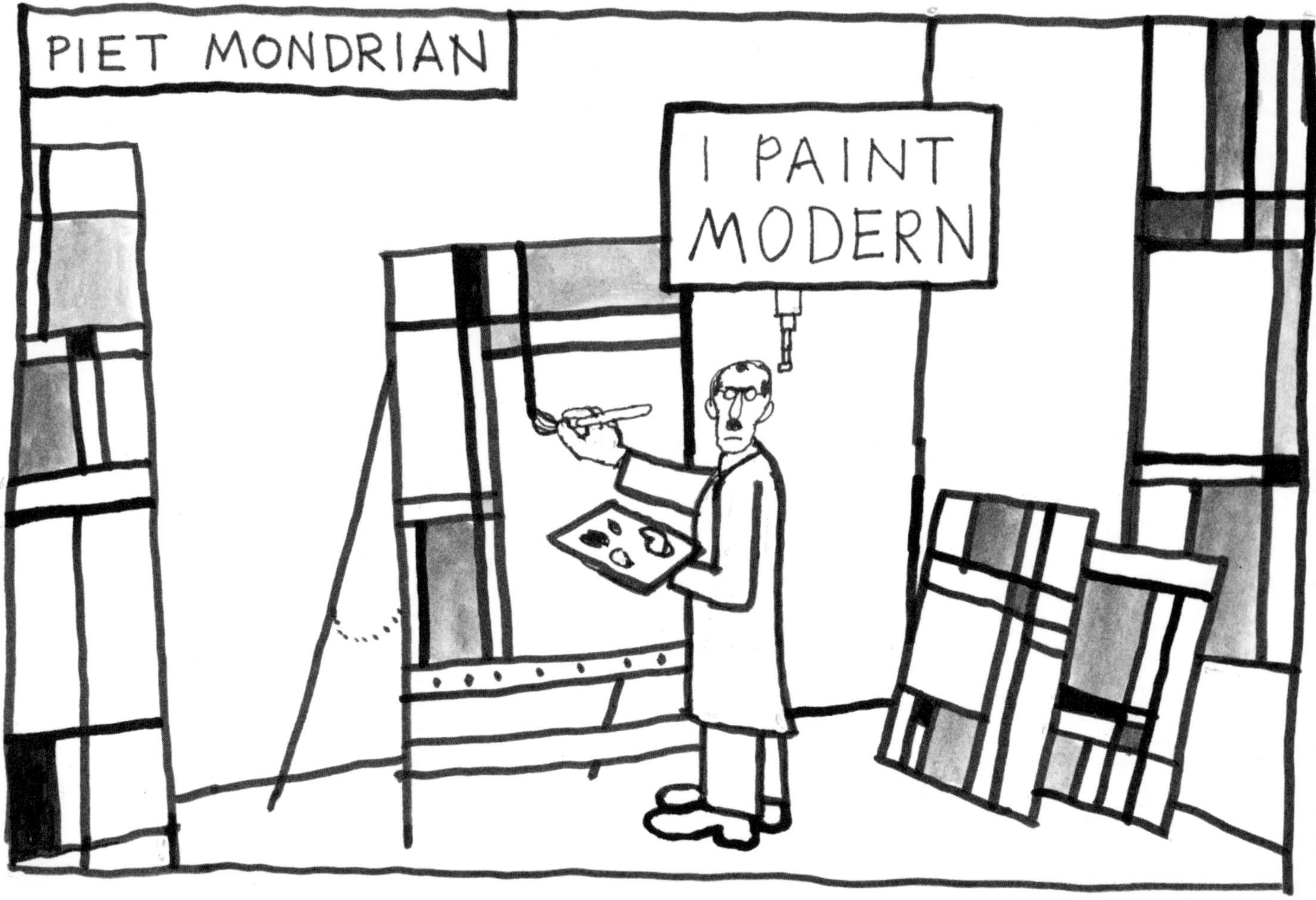
PIET MONDRIAN
I PAINT MODERN

ULYSSES S. GRANT

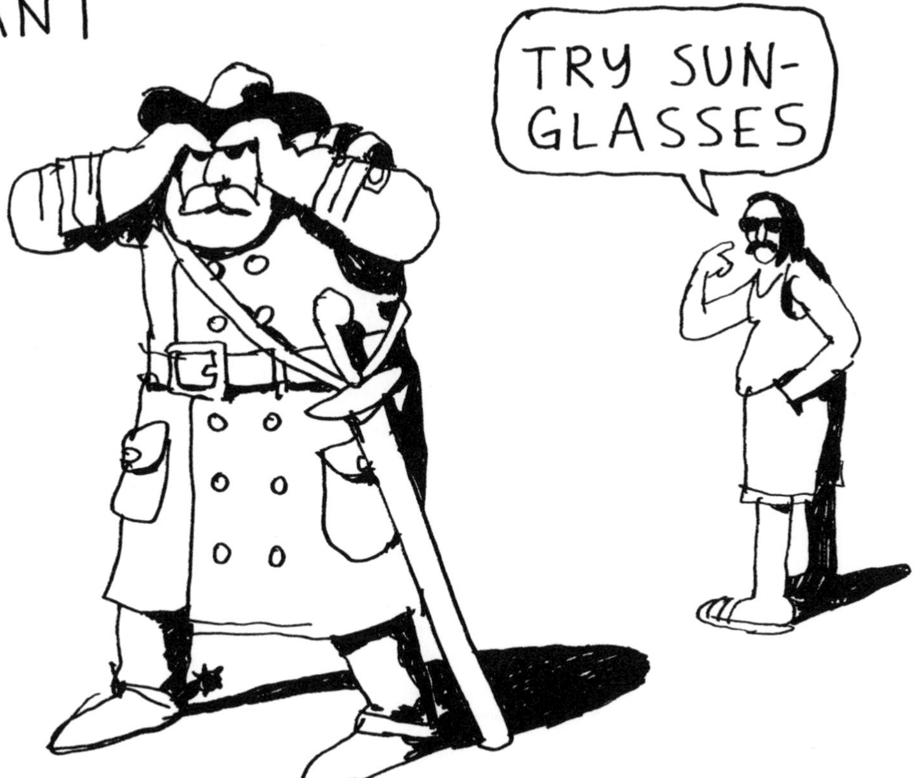
TRY SUN-GLASSES

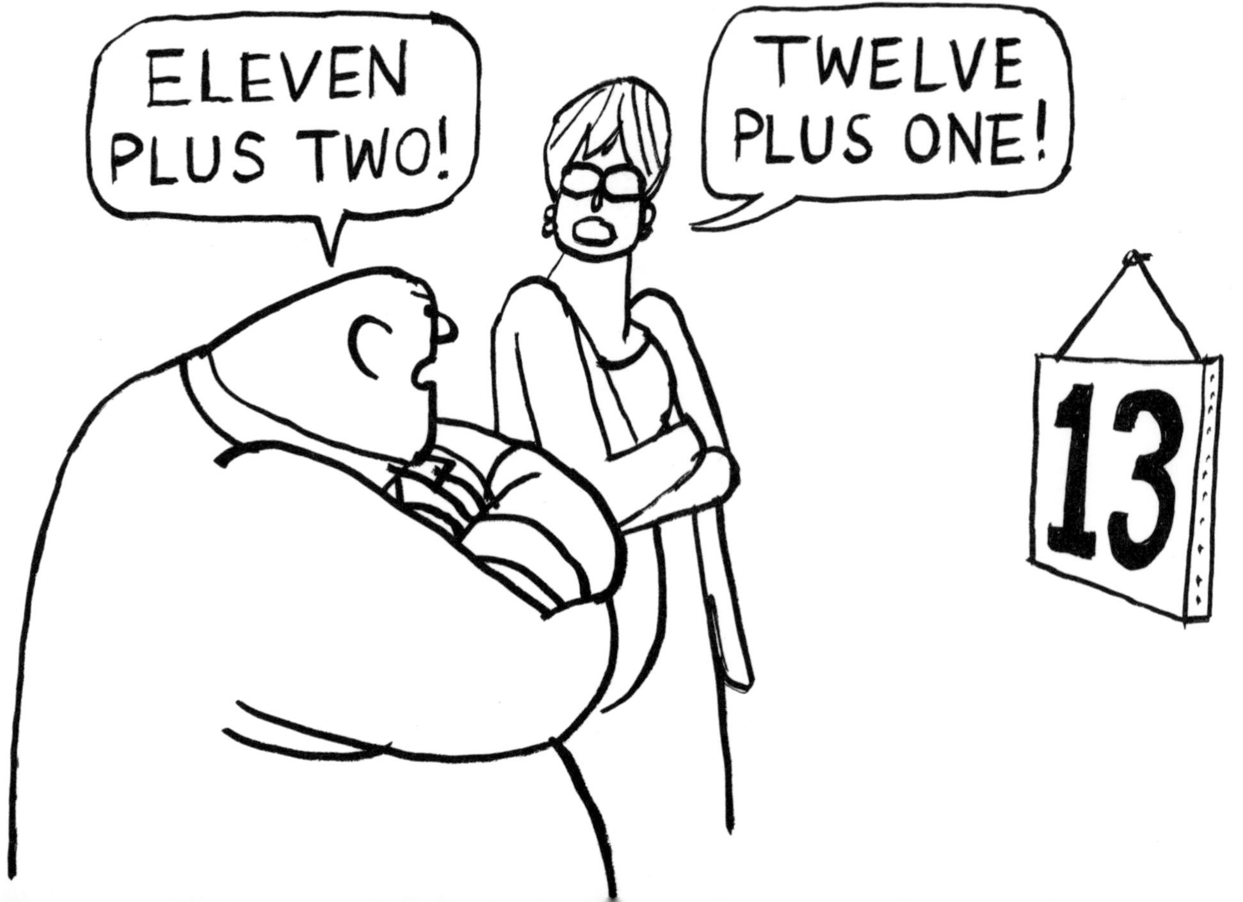
ELEVEN PLUS TWO!
TWELVE PLUS ONE!
13

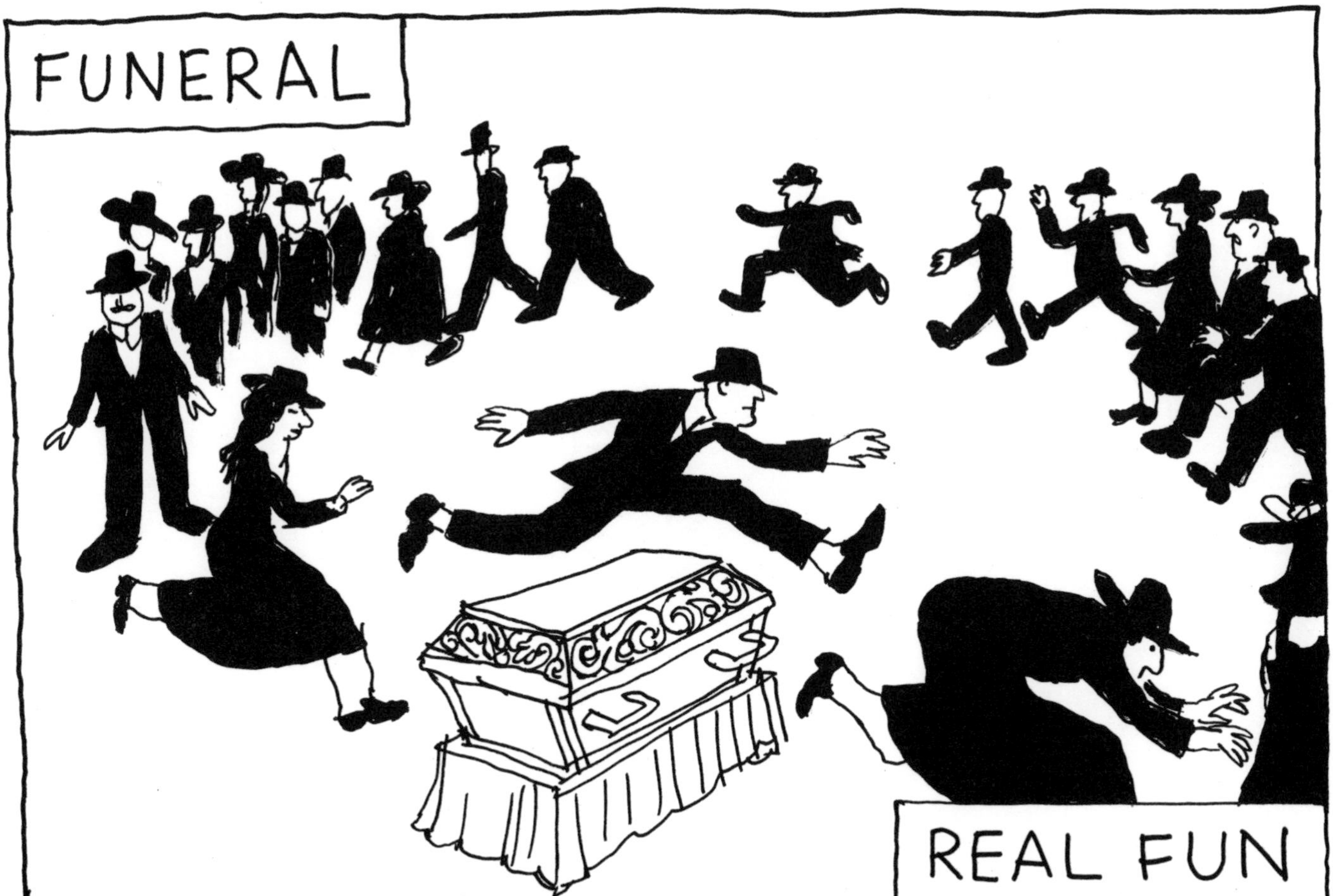
FUNERAL
REAL FUN

THE
ARCHEOLOGIST

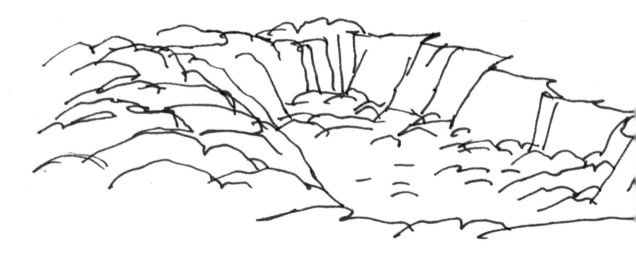

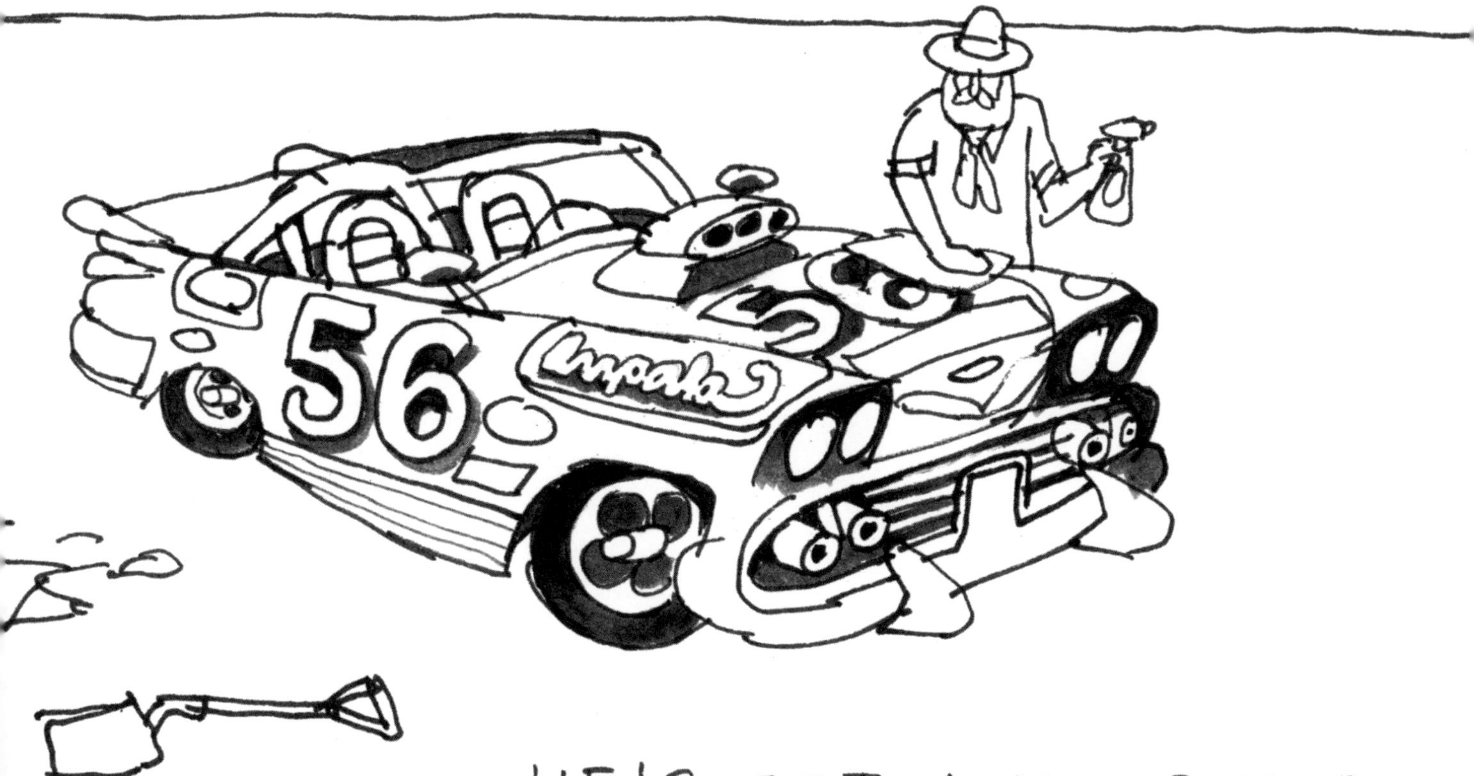
56
Impala

HE'S GOT A HOT RELIC

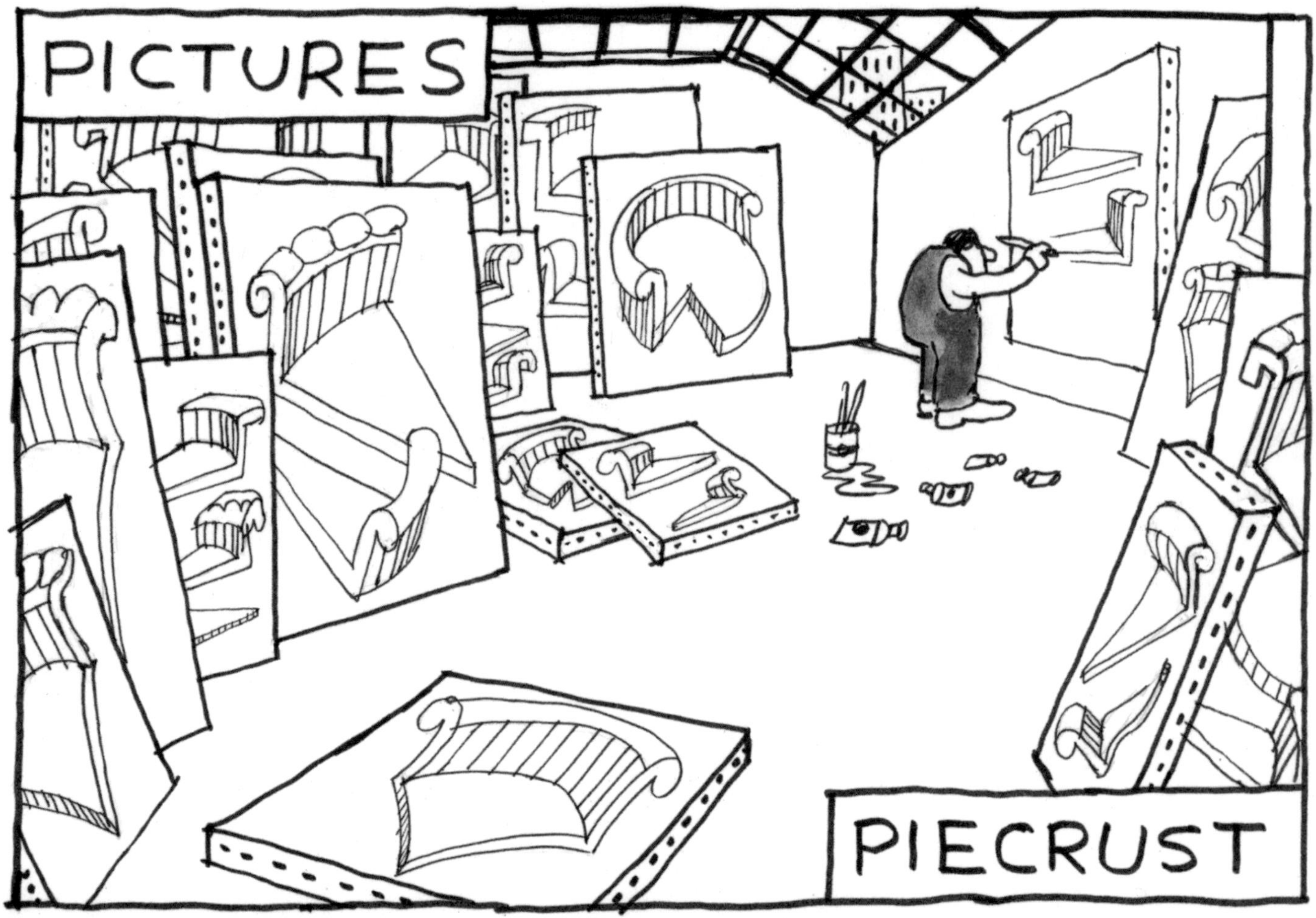
PICTURES
PIECRUST

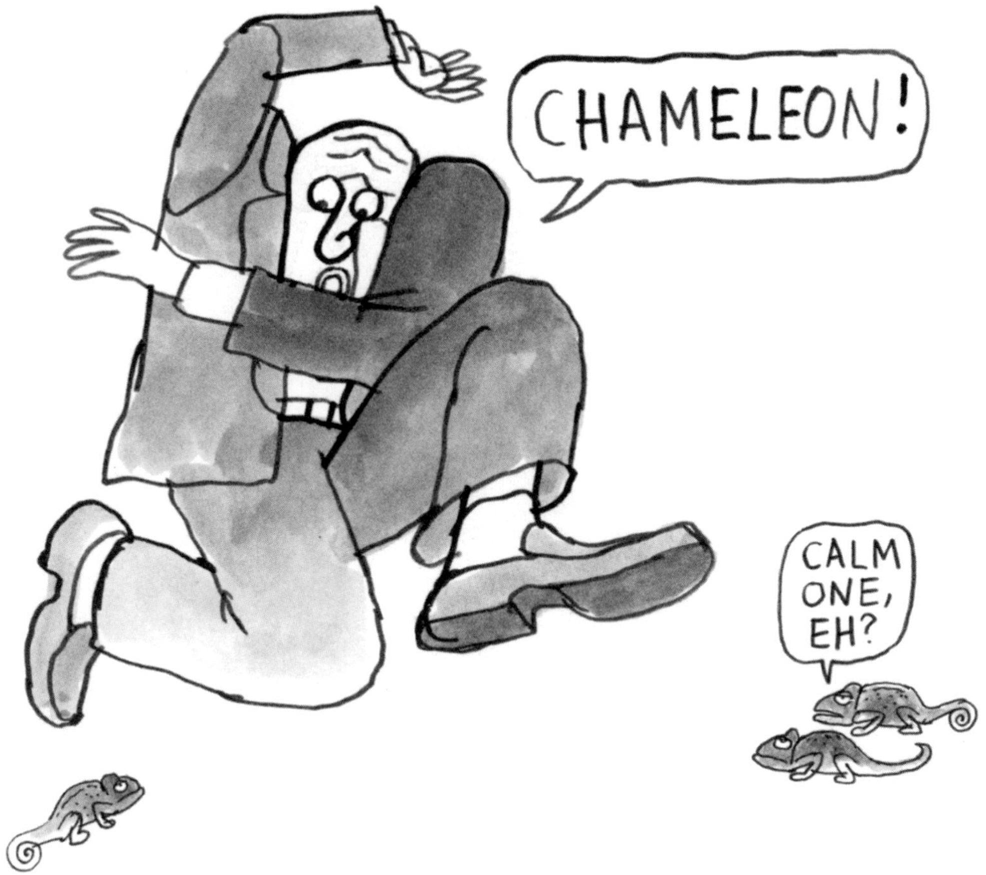
CHAMELEON!
CALM ONE, EH?

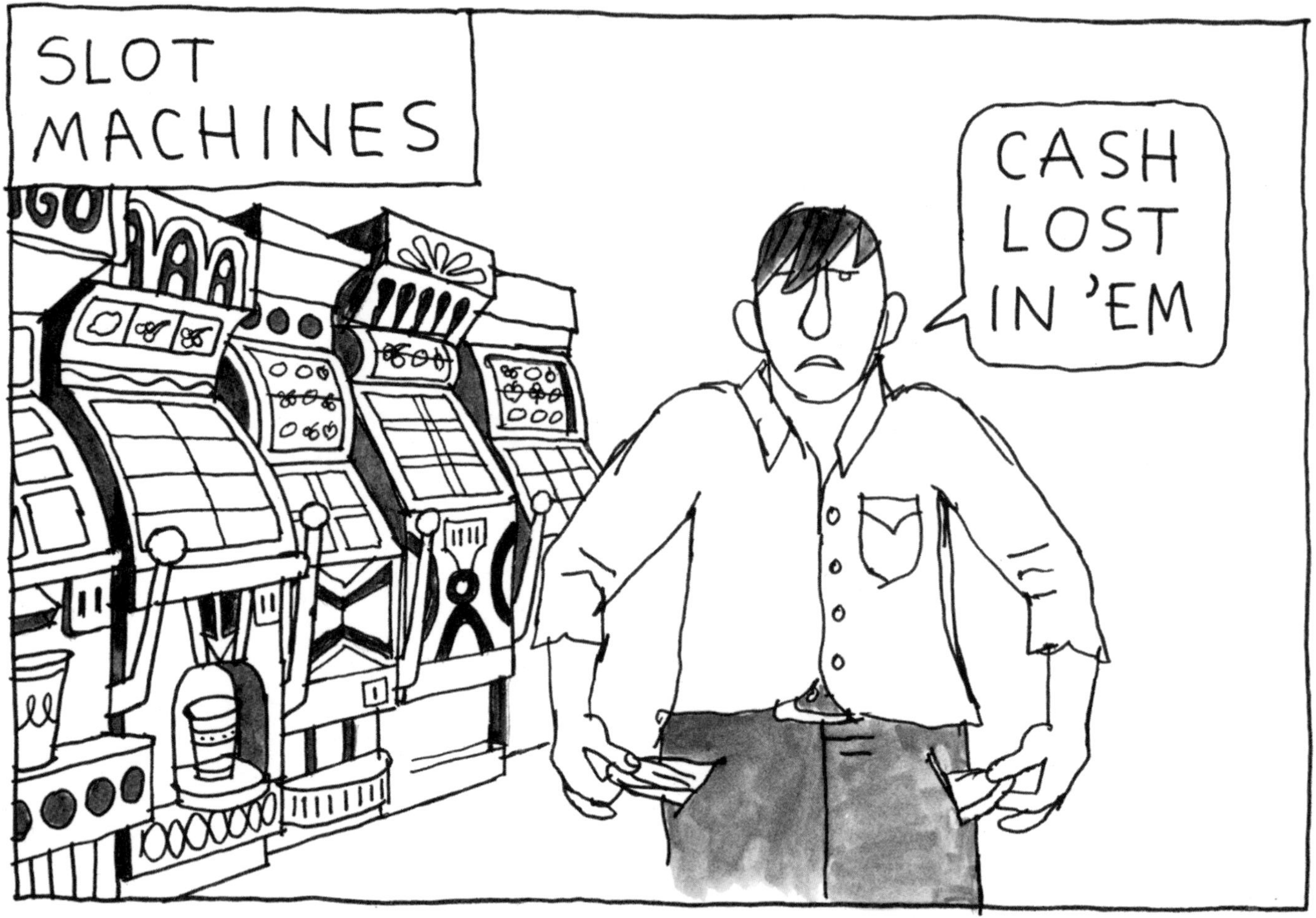
SLOT MACHINES
CASH LOST IN 'EM

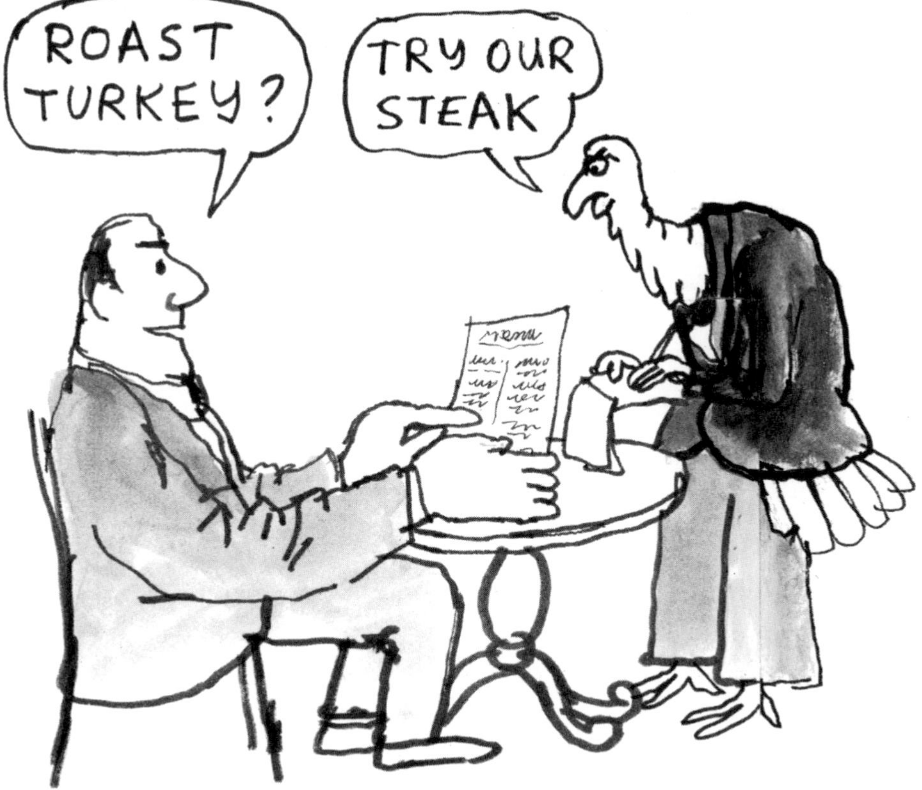
ROAST TURKEY?
TRY OUR STEAK

ESKIMOS

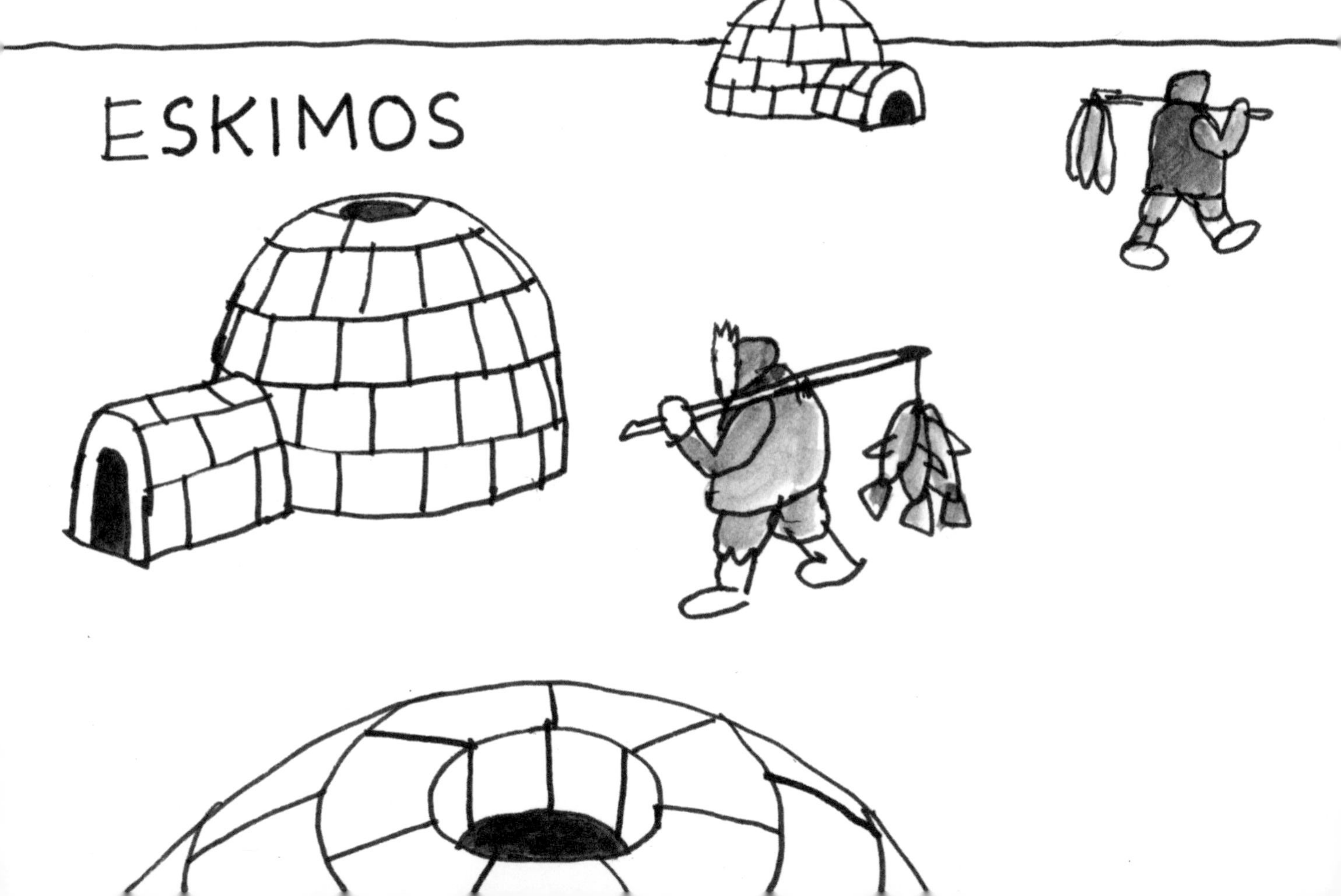

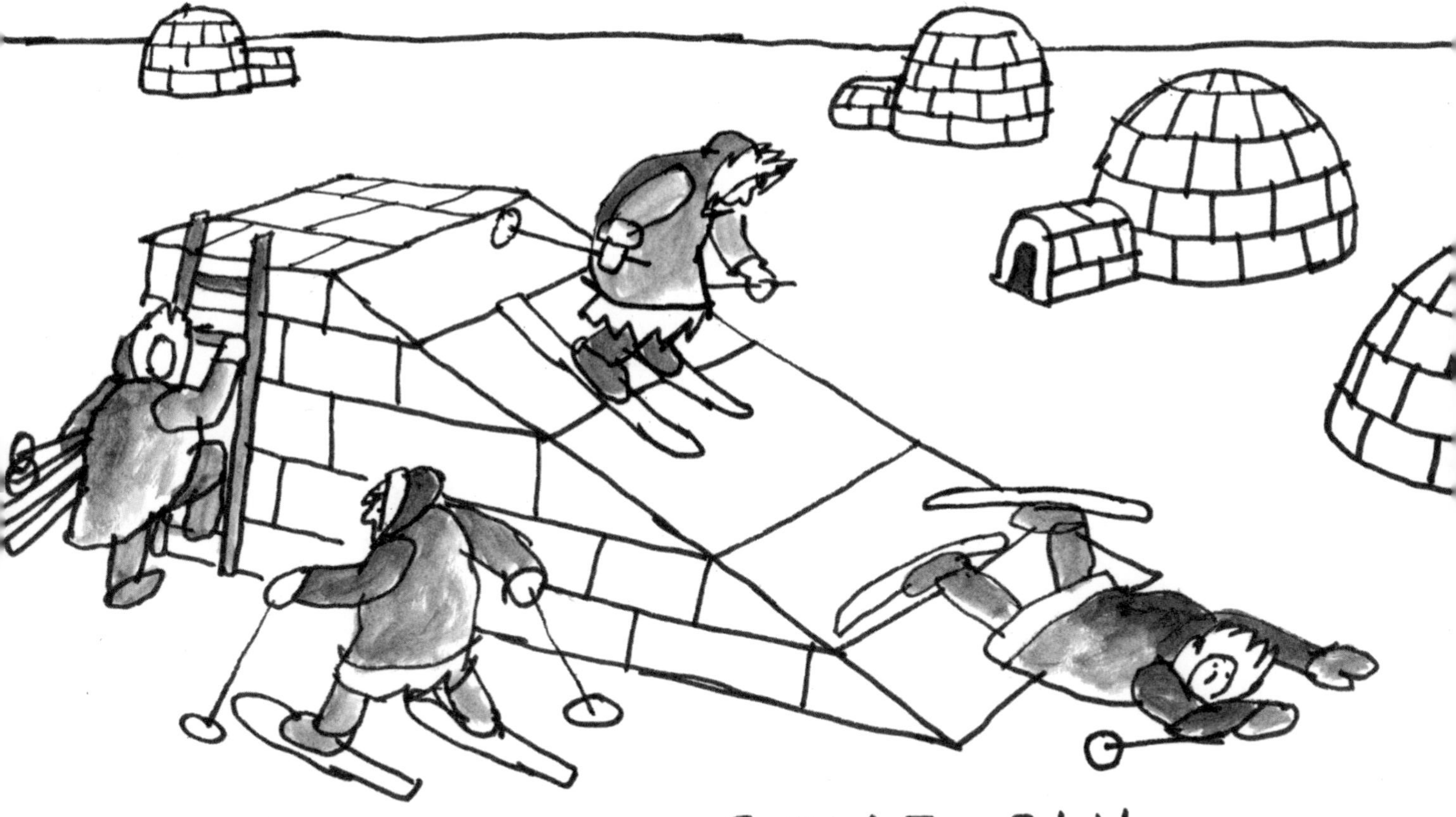

SOME SKI

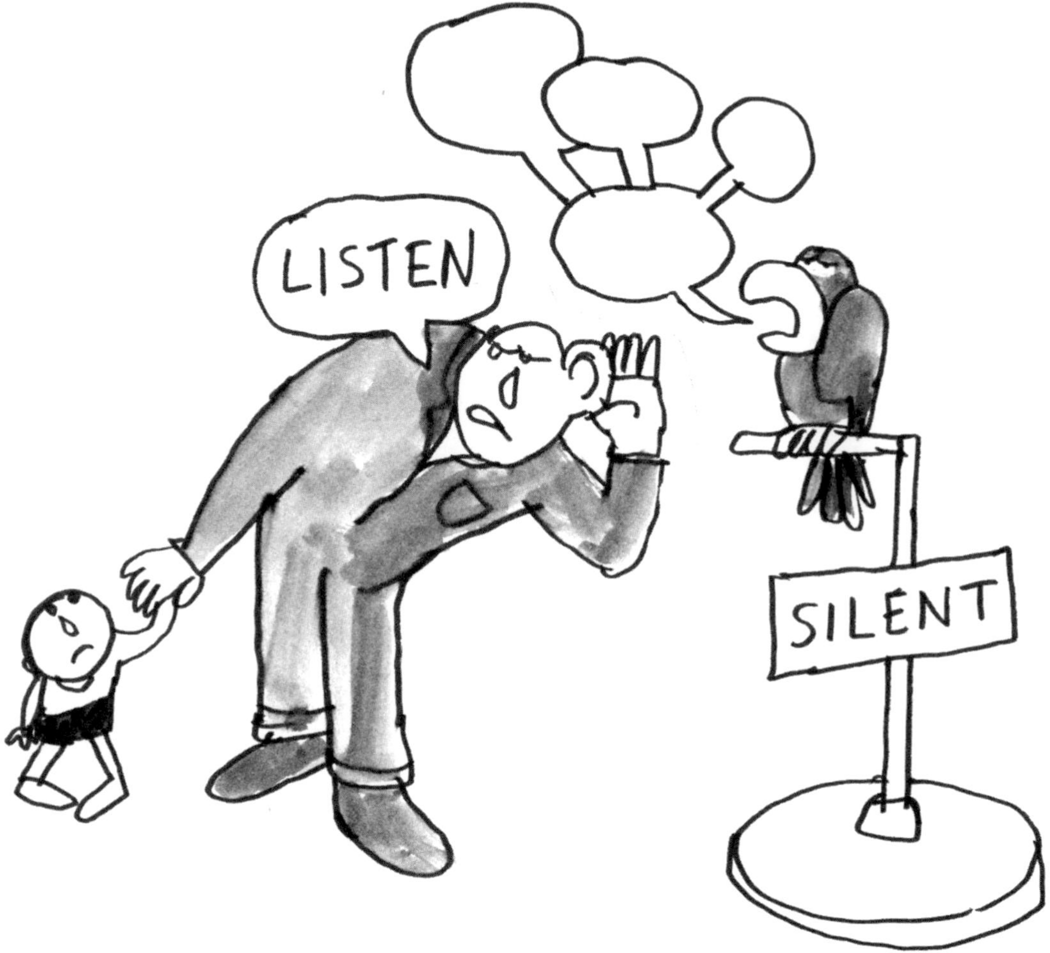
LISTEN
SILENT

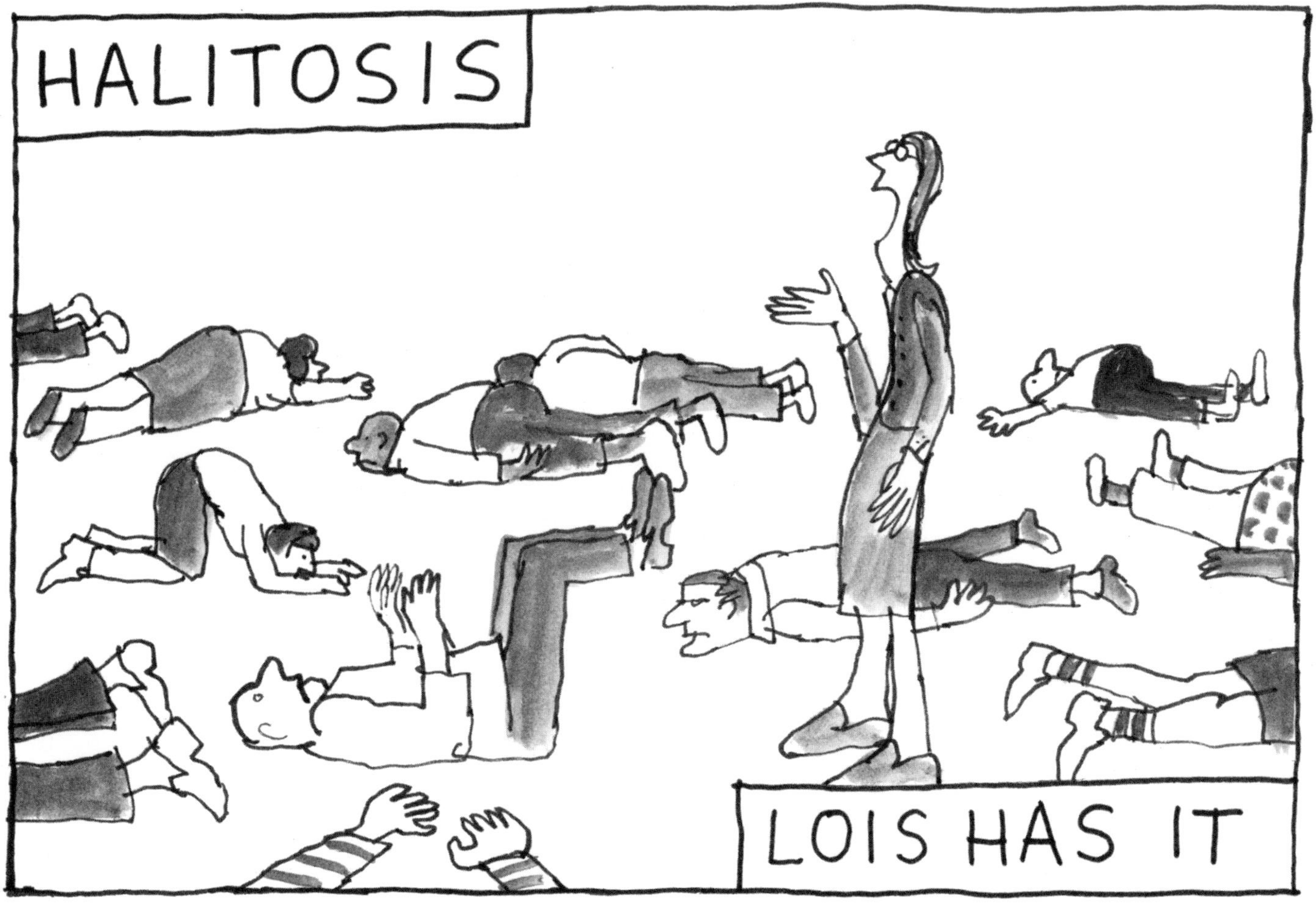
HALITOSIS
LOIS HAS IT

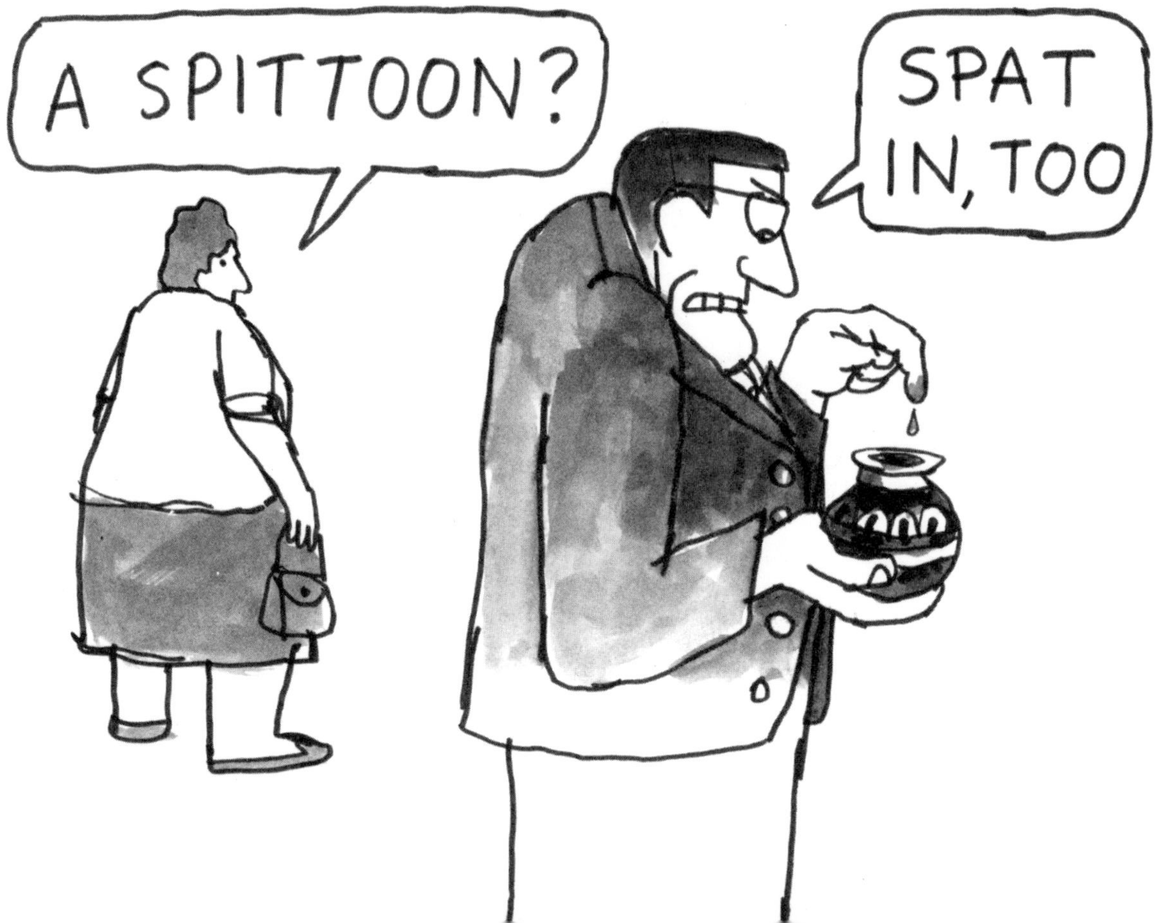
A SPITTOON?
SPAT IN, TOO

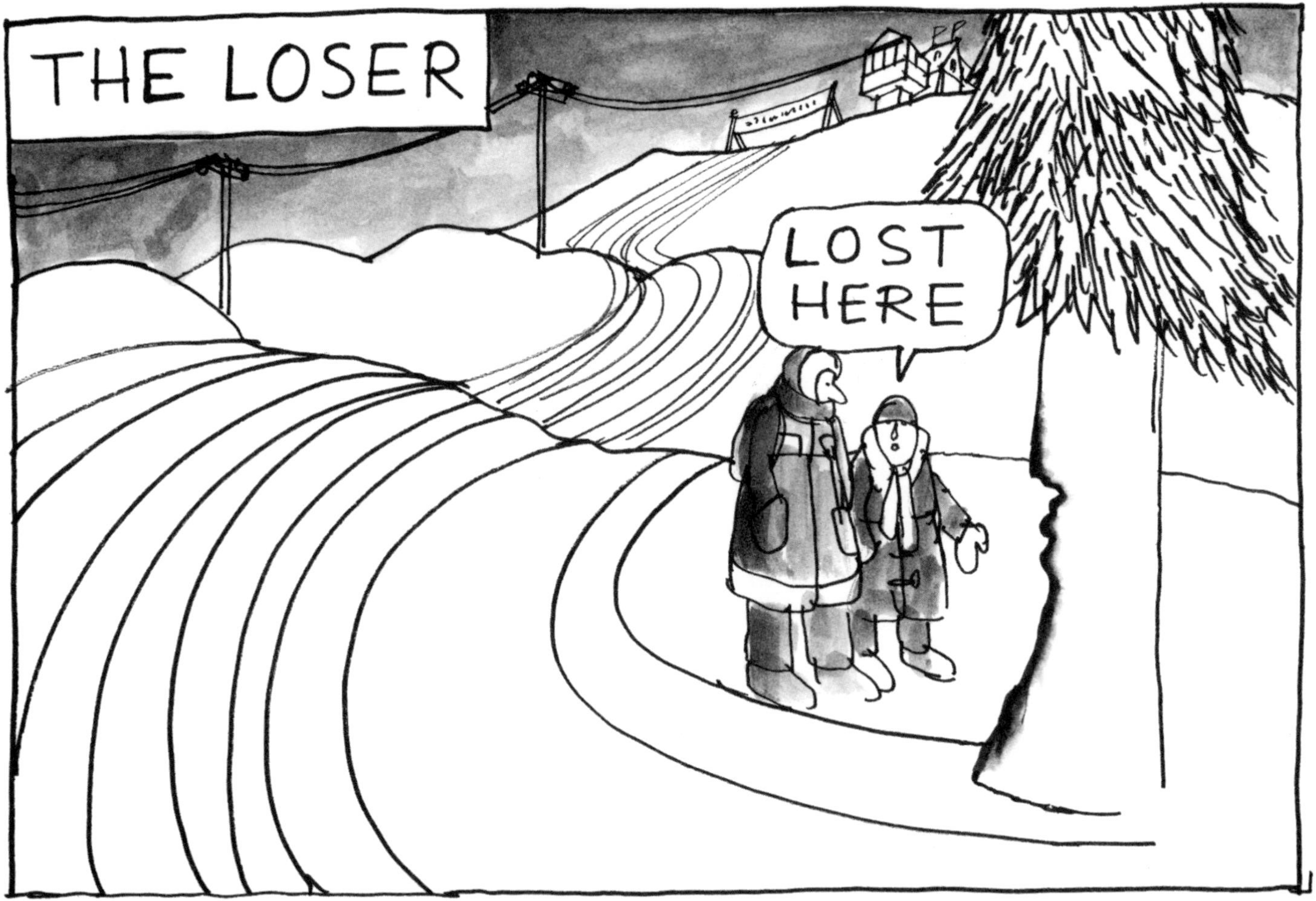
THE LOSER
LOST HERE

A PSYCHIATRIST

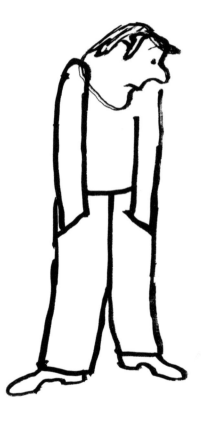

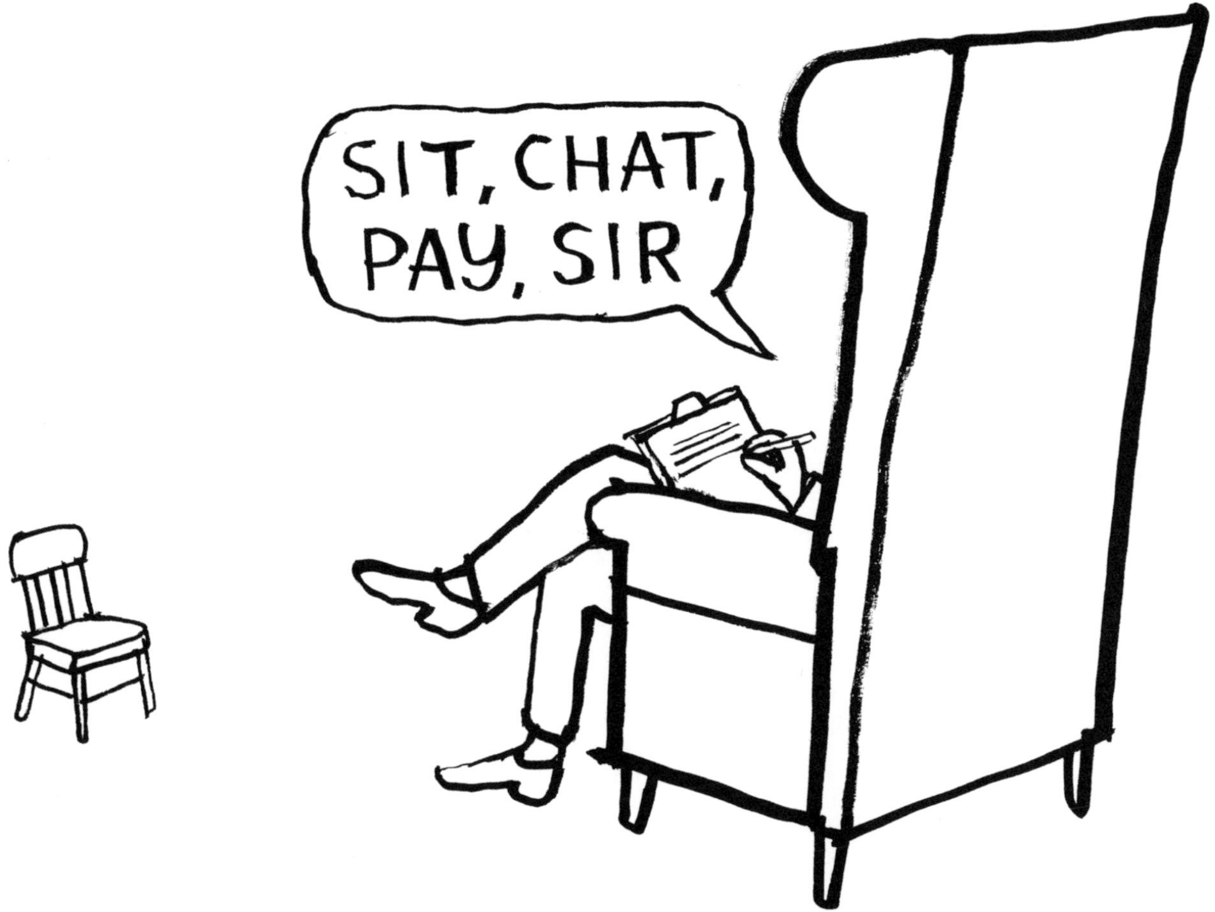
SIT, CHAT, PAY, SIR

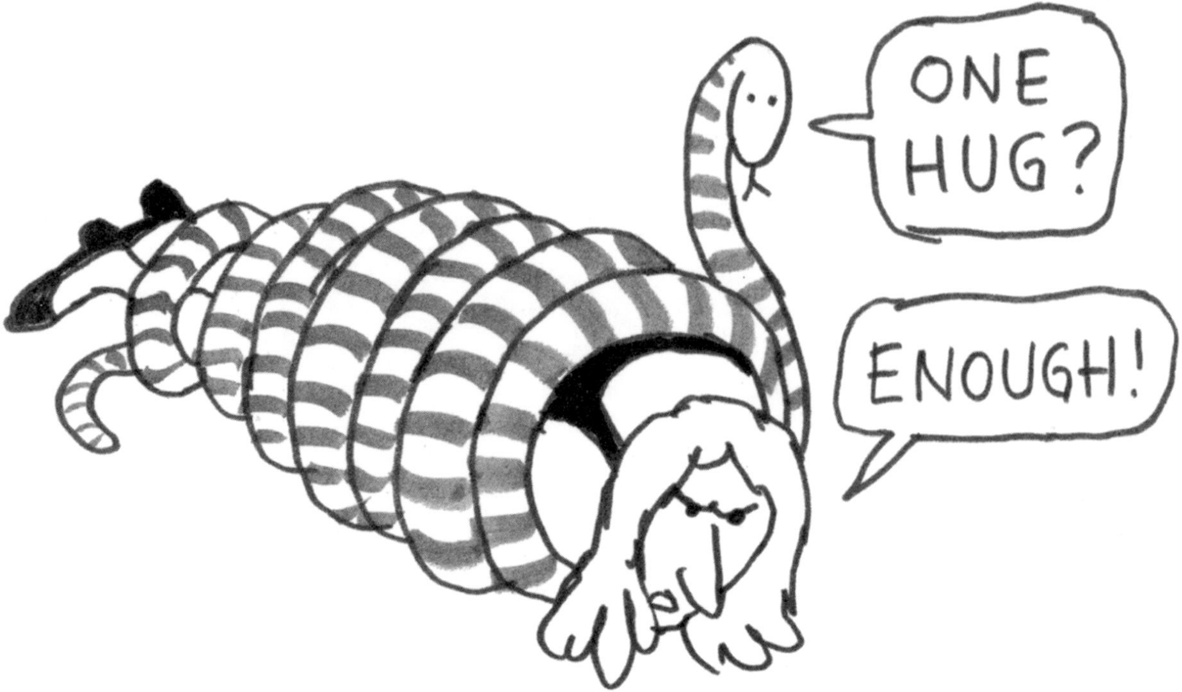
ONE HUG?
ENOUGH!

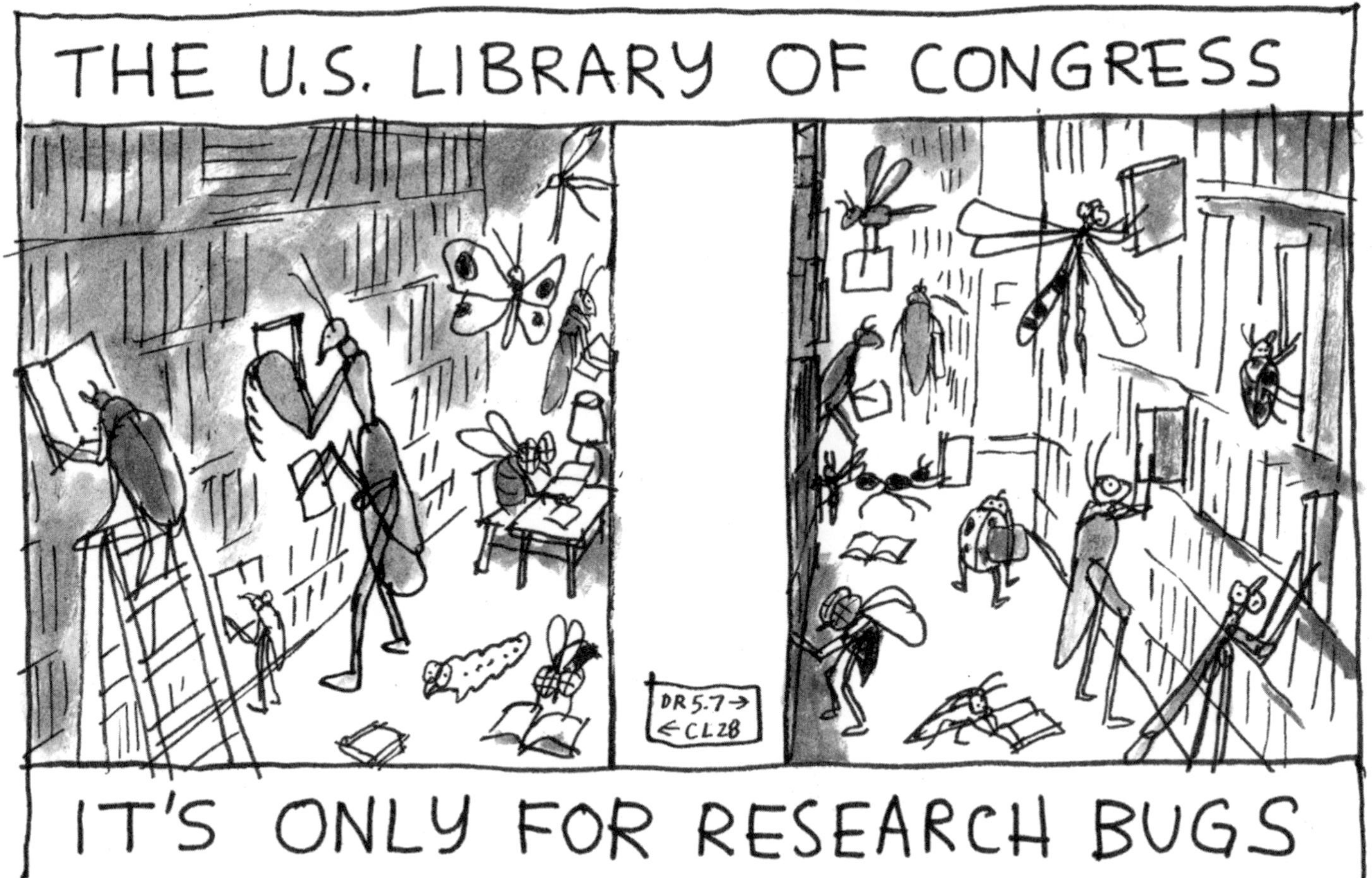
THE U.S. LIBRARY OF CONGRESS
DR 5.7 →
← CL 28
IT'S ONLY FOR RESEARCH BUGS

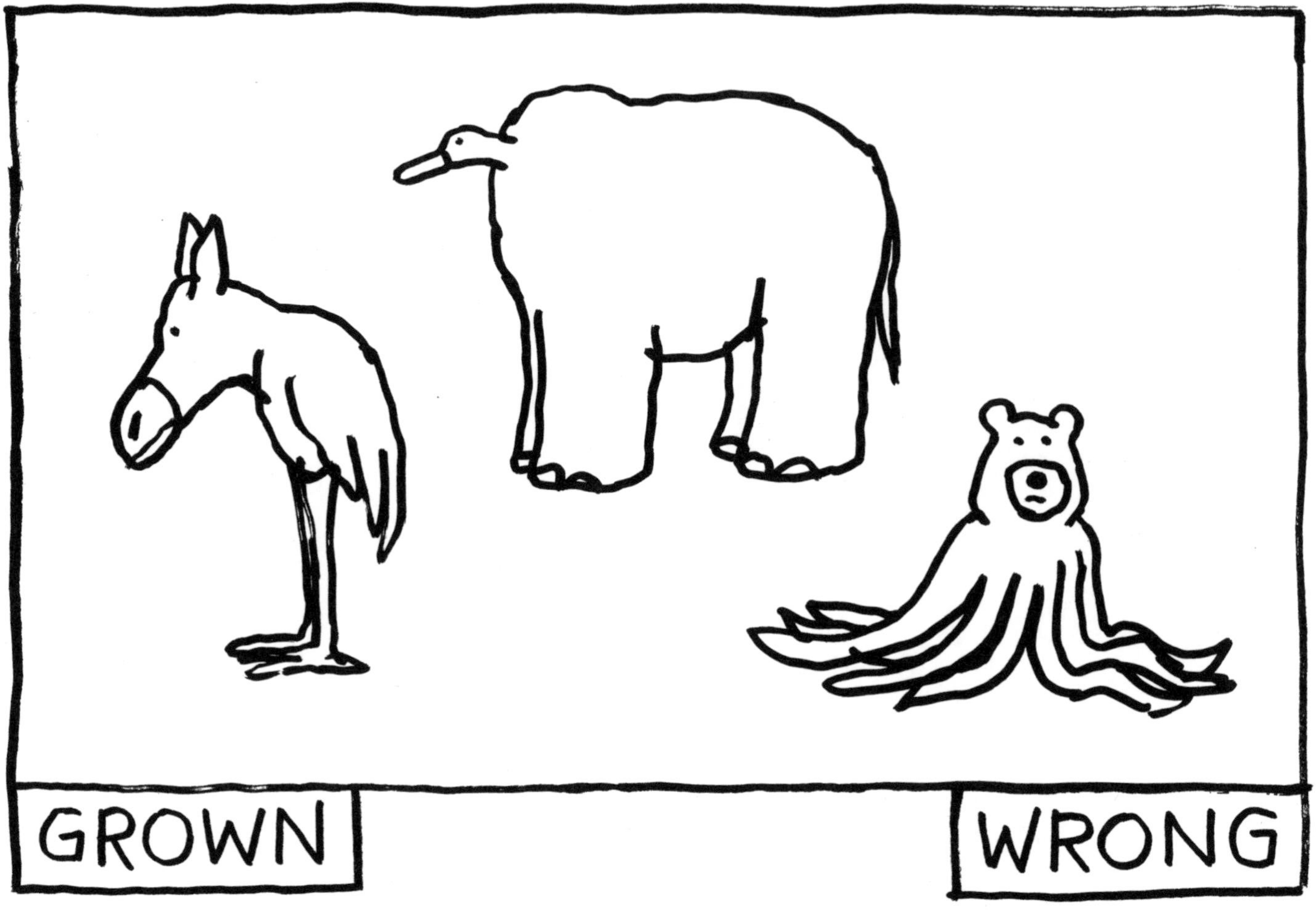
GROWN
WRONG

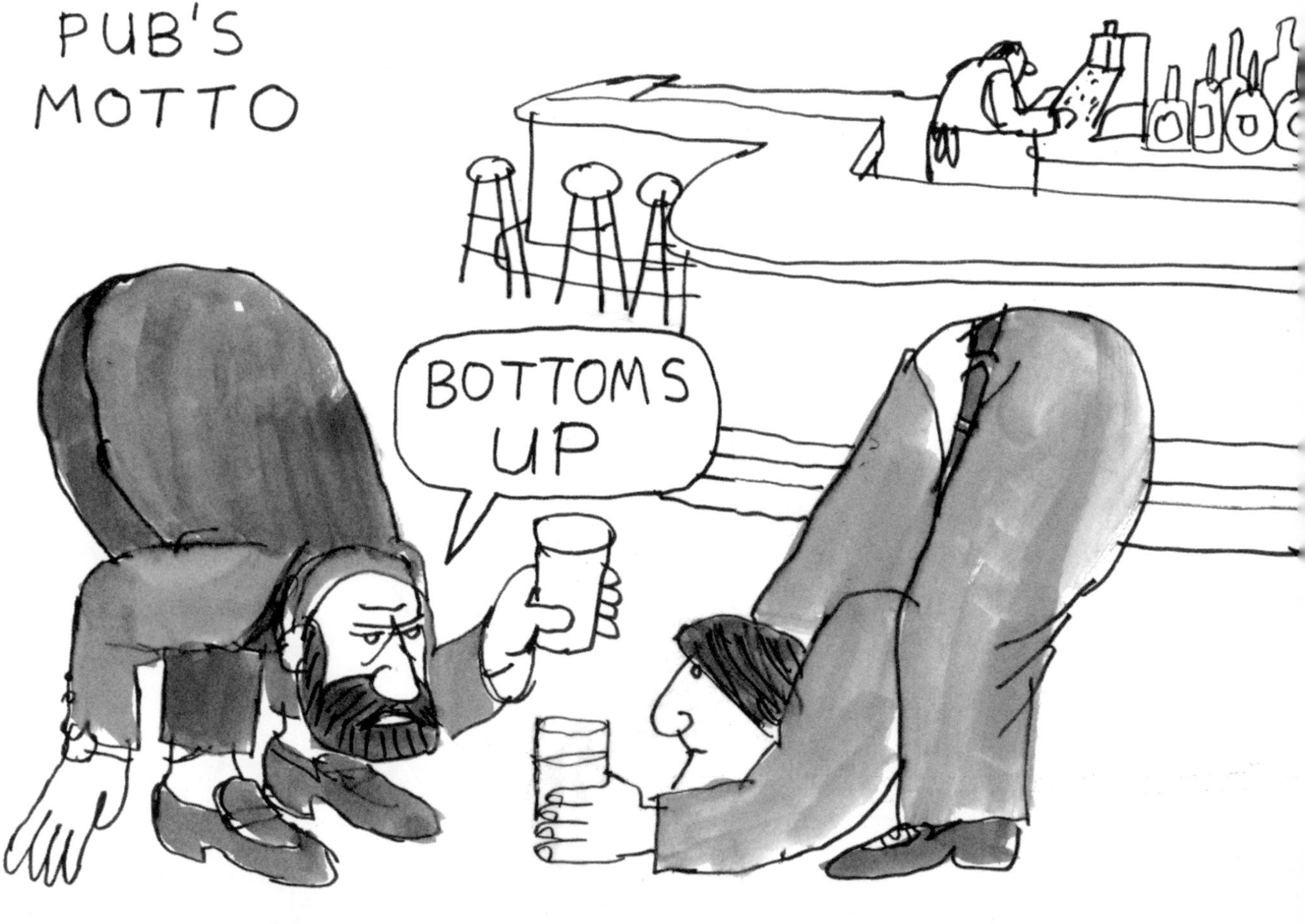
PUB'S MOTTO
BOTTOMS UP

LIFE'S AIM

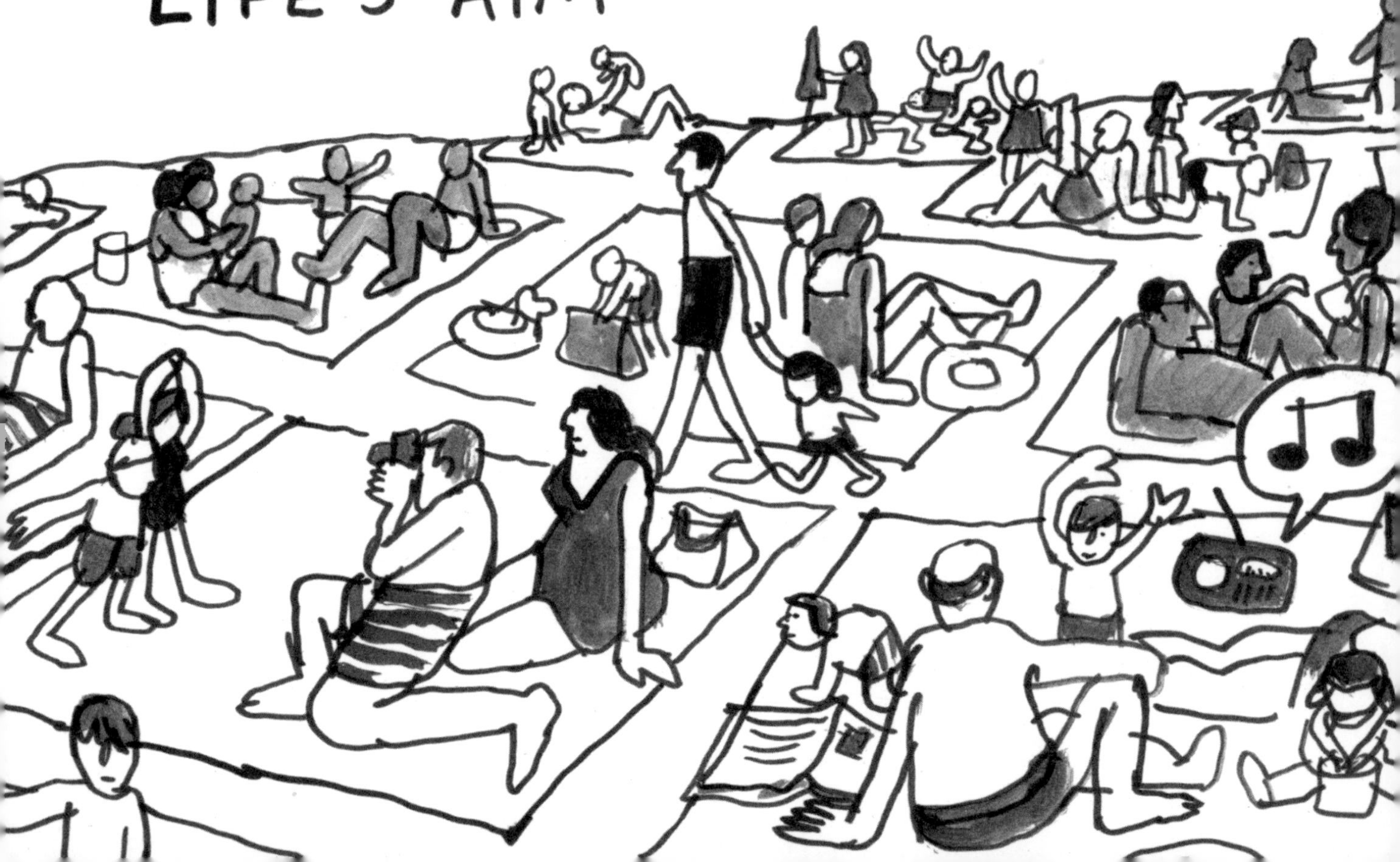

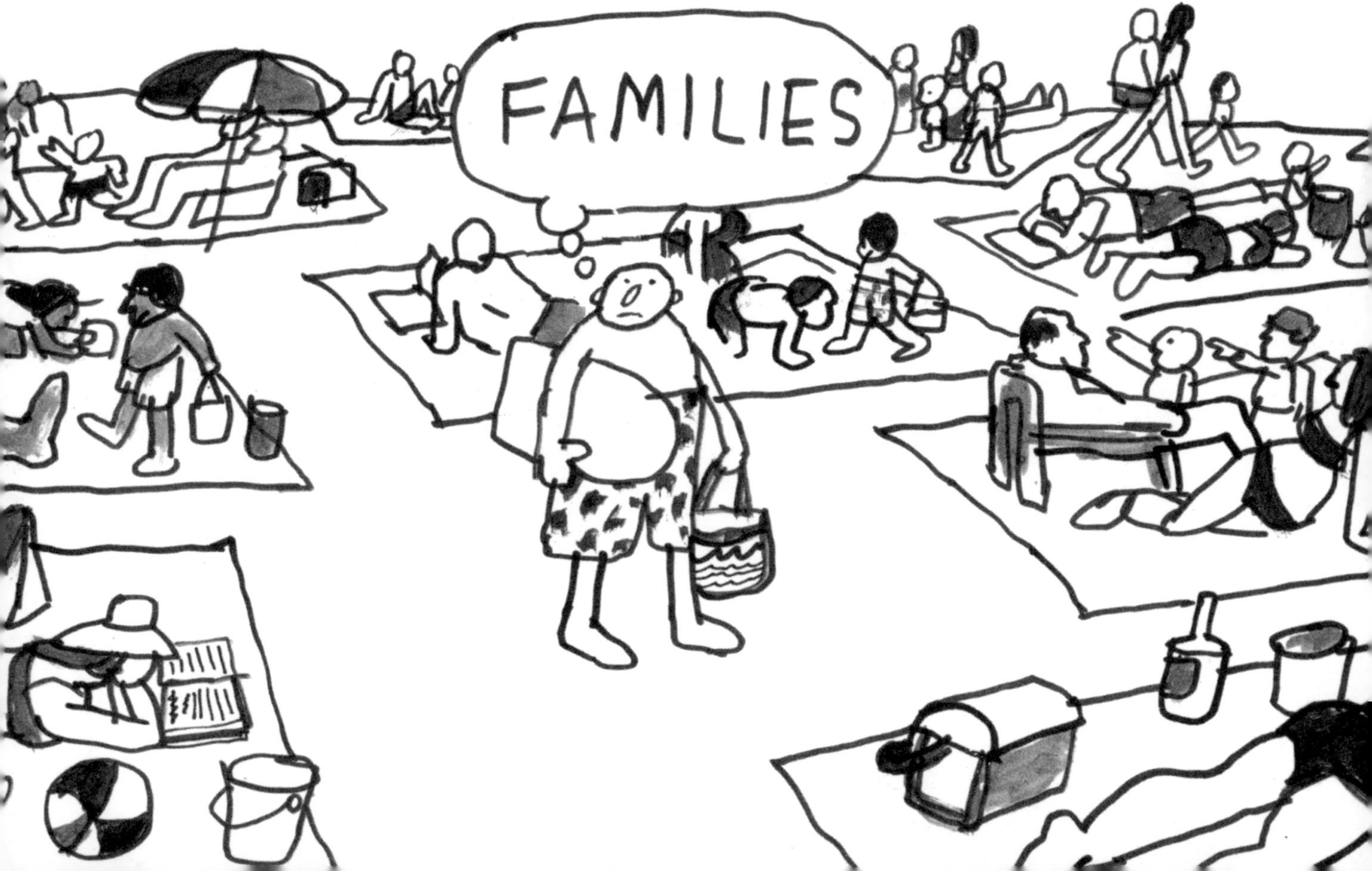
FAMILIES

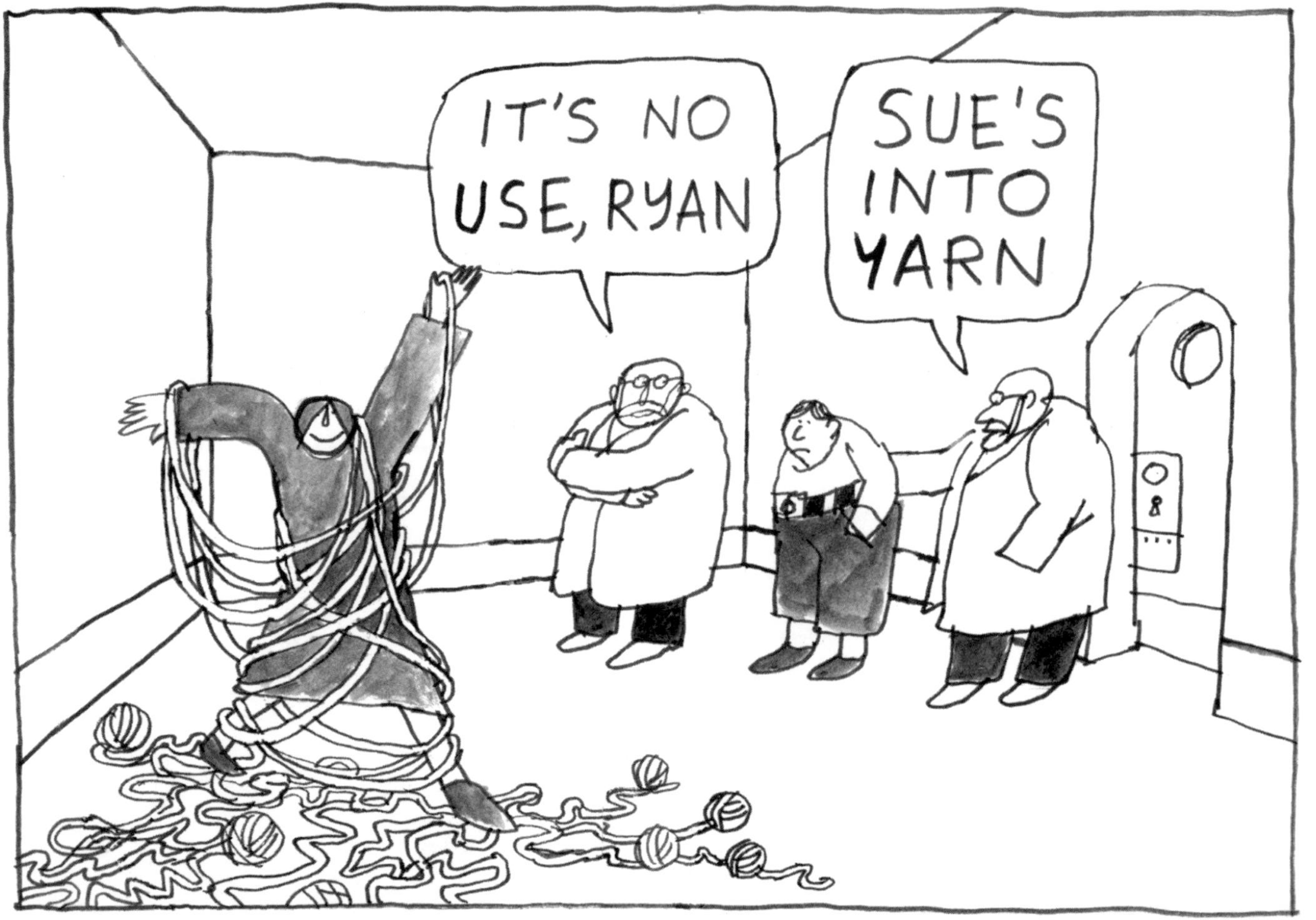
IT'S NO USE, RYAN
SUE'S INTO YARN

TELEVISION SET

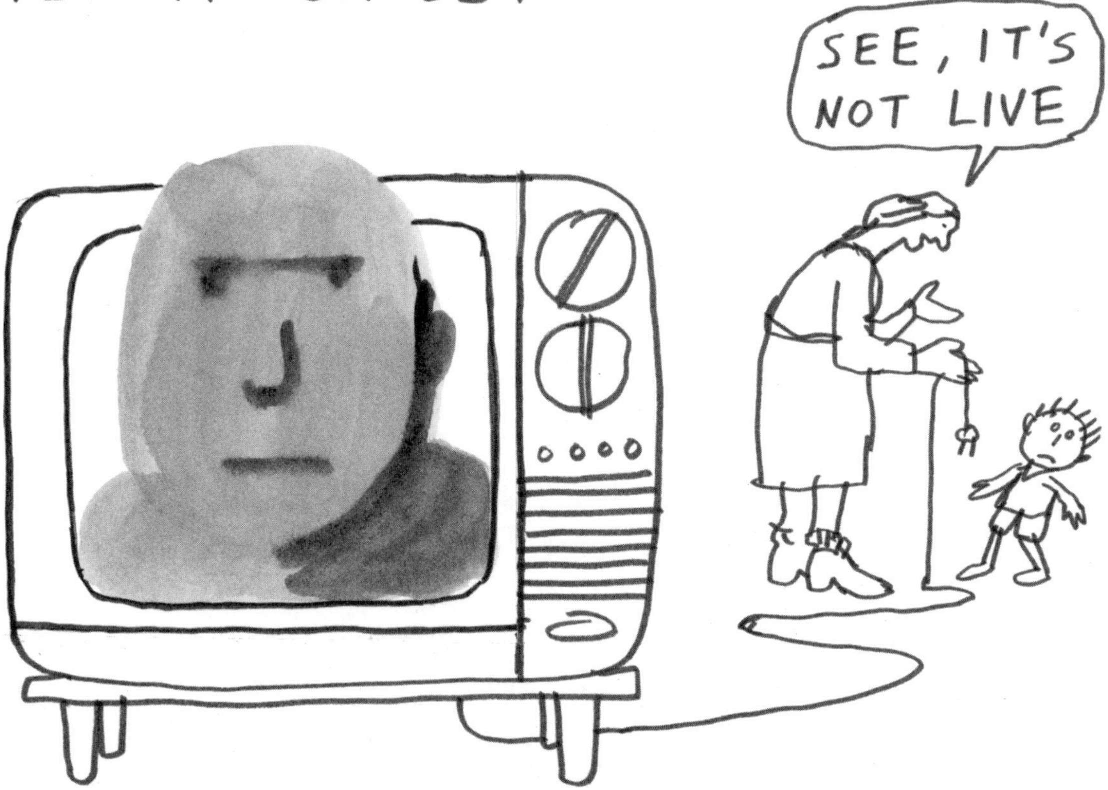
SEE, IT'S NOT LIVE

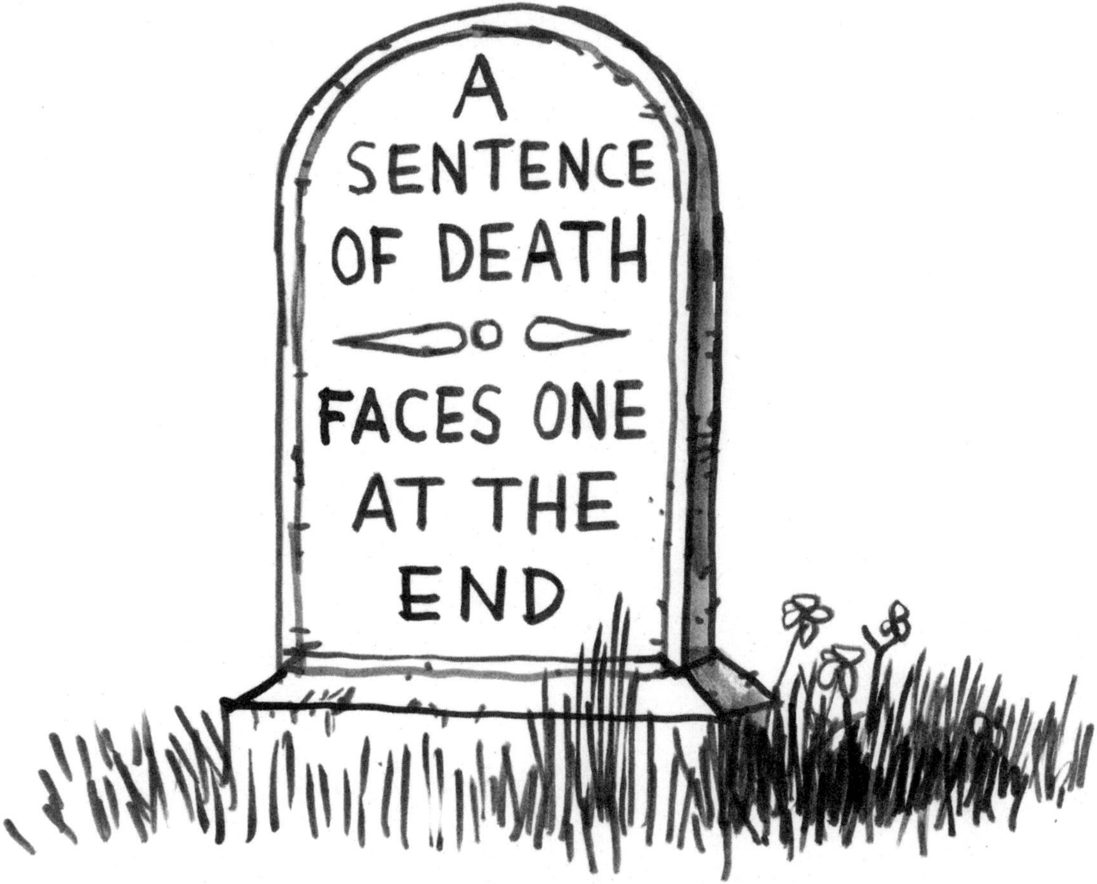
A
SENTENCE
OF DEATH
FACES ONE
AT THE
END

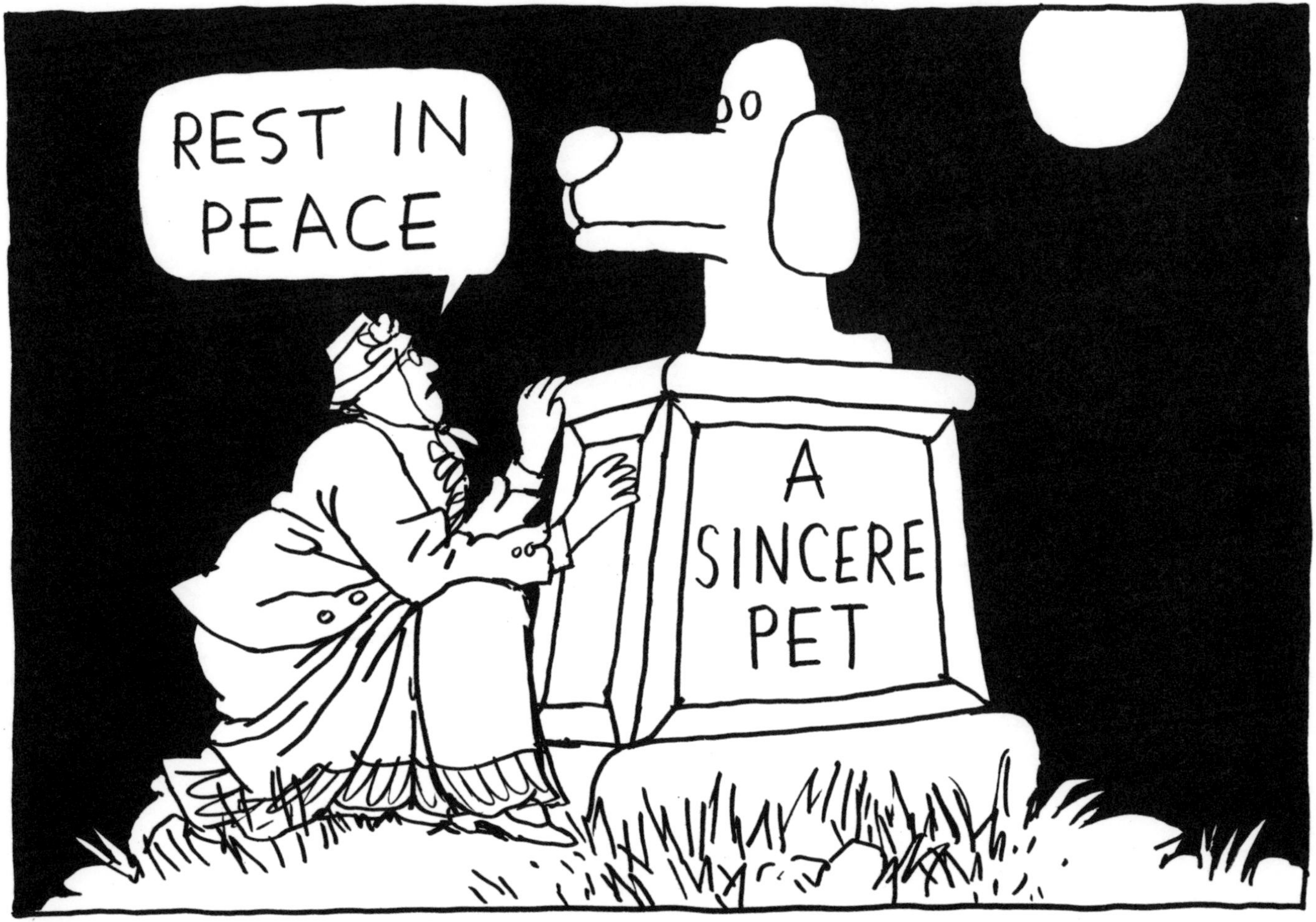
REST IN PEACE
A SINCERE PET

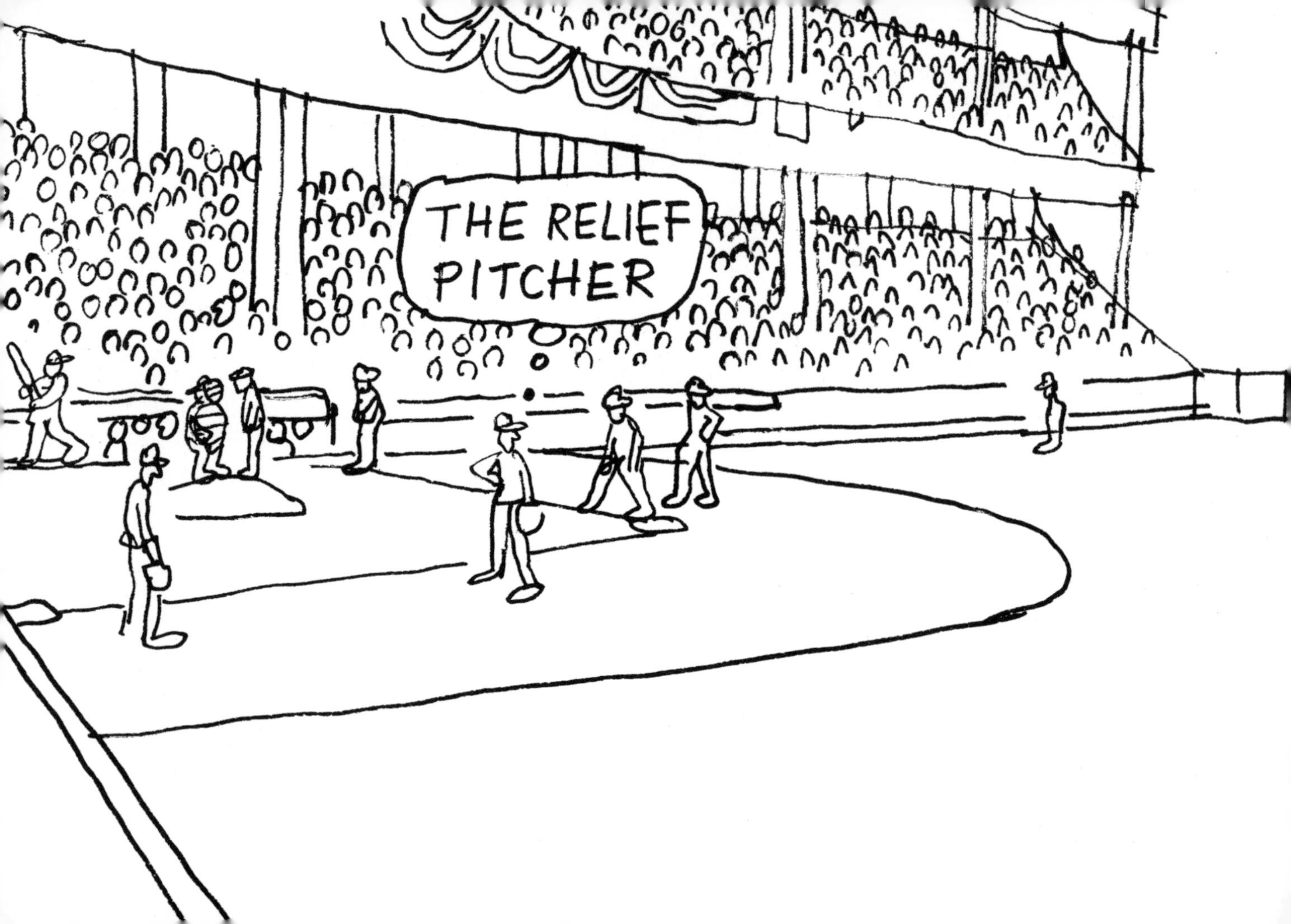
THE RELIEF PITCHER

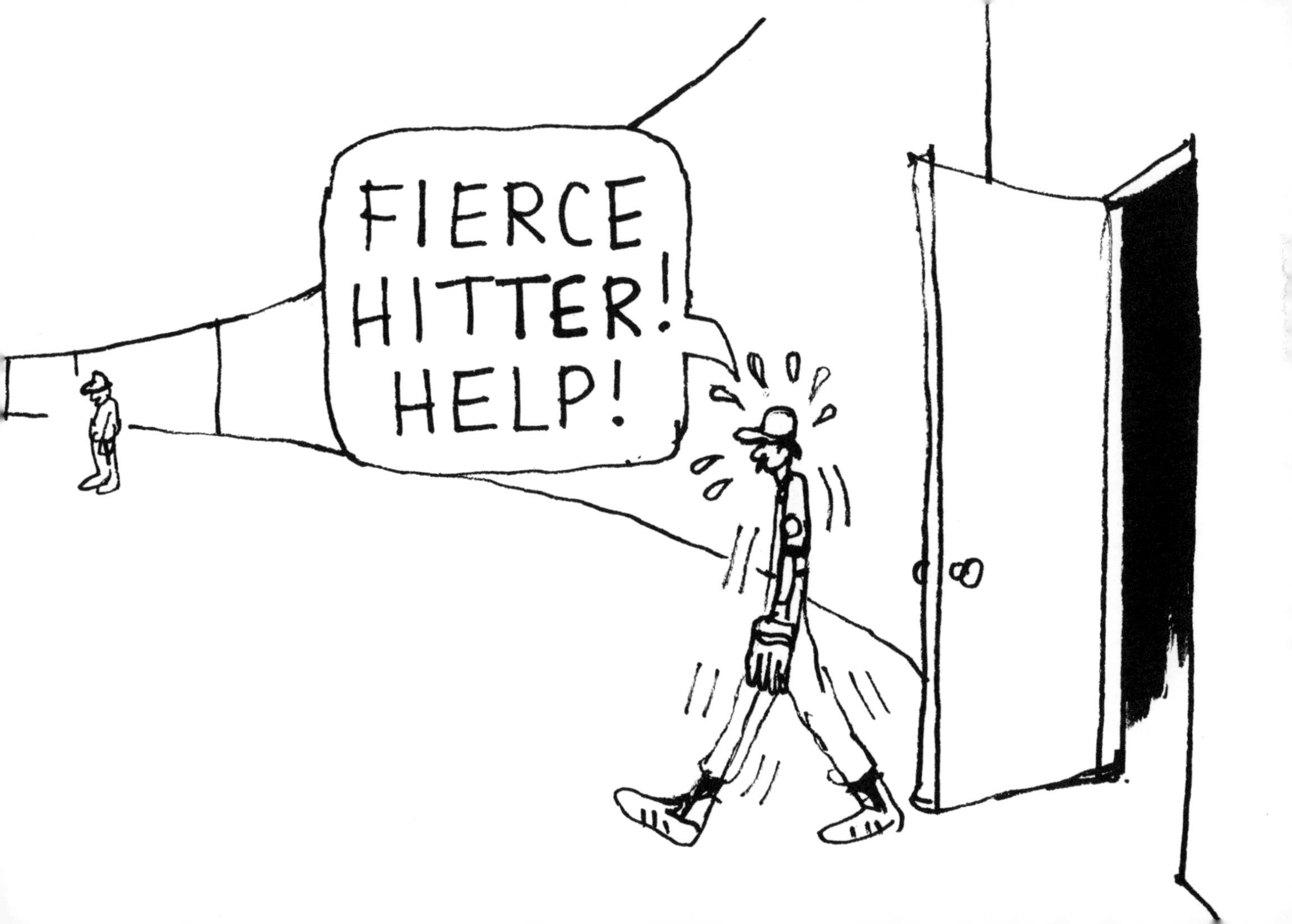
FIERCE HITTER! HELP!

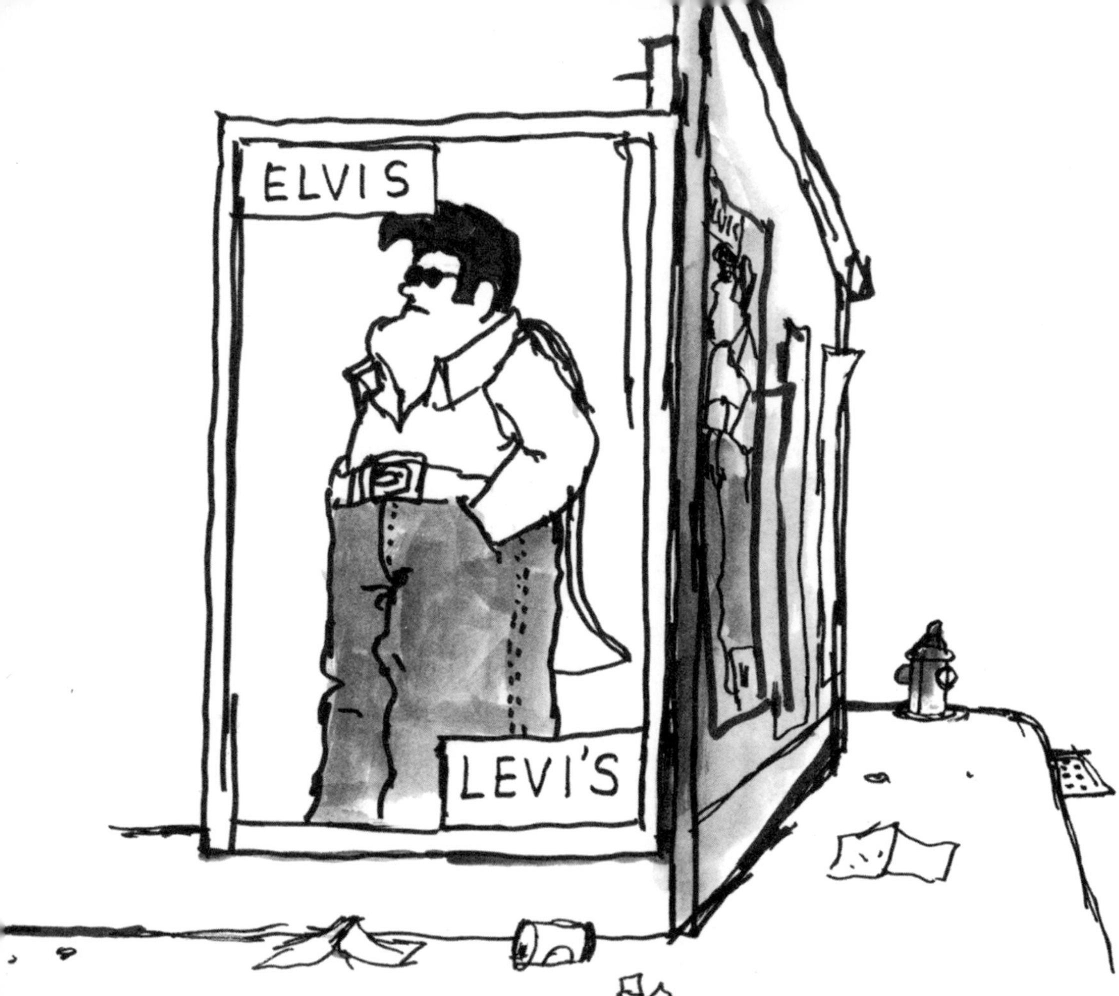
ELVIS
LEVI'S

THANK YOU VERY MUCH

Almost all of the anagrams included here were found in books, journals, or through friends. In many cases the original source of a specific anagram was unclear or unknown. Some of them were created before the twentieth century, others as recently as 1999. What follows is a list of authors with the anagram(s) they created: Josefa Heifetz Byrne (SOUTHERN CALIFORNIA/HOT SUN, OR LIFE IN A CAR); Mrs. Henry Eagleton (THE COUNTRYSIDE/NO CITY DUST HERE); Don Emmerson (LIONESSES/NOISELESS); Darryl Francis (THE U.S. LIBRARY OF CONGRESS/IT'S ONLY FOR RESEARCH BUGS); Theodore Funk (POETRY/TRY POE); William Grossman (THE EYES/THEY SEE); Robert Hooke (THE ARCHEOLOGIST/HE'S GOT A HOT RELIC); William Lawrence (A SENTENCE OF DEATH/FACES ONE AT THE END); Kathryn Ludlam (NORWEGIANS/SWEN OR INGA); E. J.

McIlvane (LIFE'S AIM/FAMILIES and COMMITTEES/COST ME TIME!); Carrol Mayors (A DECIMAL POINT?/I'M A DOT IN PLACE!); O. V. Michaelsen (ON ANY SCREEN/SEAN CONNERY?); Morton L. Mitchell (SLOT MACHINES/CASH LOST IN 'EM); Norman Nelson (THE NUDIST COLONY/NO UNTIDY CLOTHES); Laura Olkowski (SCHOOL CAFETERIA/HOT CEREAL FIASCO; LIFE ON MARS?/ALIEN FORMS!; NICE SEAT/I CAN'T SEE; and REST IN PEACE/A SINCERE PET); Arthur Pearson (ROAST TURKEY?/TRY OUR STEAK); and D. C. Ver (THE ANSWER/WASN'T HERE).

Thanks also to John Baumann, my aunt Rena, O. V. Michaelsen for providing most of the author credits, Laura Olkowski, Mark Saltveit, Will Shortz, and John D. Williams, Jr., the executive director of the Scrabble Association, for suggesting this book in the first place.

BIBLIOGRAPHY

Charles Carroll Bombaugh, *Oddities and Curiosities of Words and Literature* (New York: Dover Publications, 1961); Dmitri Borgmann, *Language on Vacation: An Olio of Orthographical Oddities* (New York: Scribner, 1965); A. Ross Eckler, *Making the Alphabet Dance* (New York: St. Martin's Press, 1996); R. J. Edwards, *The Longman Anagram Dictionary* (Essex, England: Longman, 1985); Willard Espy, *Garden of Eloquence: A Rhetorical Bestiary* (New York: Harper & Row, 1983) and *An Almanac of Words at Play* (New York: Clarkson N. Potter, 1975); Patrick Hughes, *Words at Play* from *The Paradox Box* (Boston: Redstone Press, 1993); O. V. Michaelsen, *Words at Play: Quips, Quirks & Oddities* (New York: Sterling Publishing Co., 1997).

*To Pete Cowdin and Deb Pettid

Levi's is a registered trademark.

Copyright © 2000 by Jon Agee. All rights reserved. Distributed in Canada by Douglas & McIntyre Ltd.
Printed in the United States of America
First edition, 2000
12 11 10 9 8 7 6 5 4 3 2

Library of Congress Cataloging-in-Publication Data
Agee, Jon.
    Elvis lives! : and other anagrams / Jon Agee.
        p.   cm.
    ISBN 0-374-32127-2
    1. Anagrams.   I. Title.
    PN6371.5.A335   2000
    793.734—dc21   99-38139